Now...a
Harlequin
romance
by Anne Mather
comes to life
on the movie screen

starring
KEIR DULLEA · SUSAN PENHALIGON

Leopard in the Snow

Guest Stars
KENNETH MORE · BILLIE WHITELAW

featuring GORDON THOMSON as MICHAEL
and JEREMY KEMP as BOLT

Produced by JOHN QUESTED and CHRIS HARROP
Screenplay by ANNE MATHER and JILL HYEM
Directed by GERRY O'HARA

An Anglo-Canadian Co-Production

Flamingo Moon

by

MARGARET PARGETER

Harlequin Books

TORONTO • LONDON • NEW YORK • AMSTERDAM • SYDNEY

Original hardcover edition published in 1977
by Mills & Boon Limited

ISBN 0-373-02140-2

Harlequin edition published February 1978

PRINTED IN U.S.A.

CHAPTER ONE

CÉLÈSTE had said not to come to the farm, and now that she was actually here, standing in front of it, Eve Reston began to wish she had taken her advice and stayed away. It probably wouldn't have strained the last remnants of her patience overmuch to have remained at the hotel a little longer in the hope that Céleste would eventually contact her. The DuBare ranch, or *manade*, as such places were called in the Camargue area of France, had a singularly formidable look about it, an air of distinct hostility which seemed to linger around its heat-hazed precincts. If there had been notices posted stating that strangers were unwelcome, Eve wouldn't have been at all surprised!

She had left her car beside a cluster of low scrub, a short distance behind her near the road. Why, she had no very clear idea as she certainly felt quite vulnerable without it, and half hidden as it was, it definitely wasn't handy for a quick getaway should the need arise. Maybe instinctively she had known the necessity for a more silent approach than a noisy little engine allowed.

The car she had hired from Mrs Wood, the hotel proprietress, who had owned and ran the large establishment with the help of a competent staff since her husband died. An enterprising woman who also kept a small fleet of cars which she rented to guests who came without one.

Eve was aware that Mrs Wood's curiosity was probably no greater than any other hotelier's would have been regarding a young English girl who appeared to do nothing but sit in her room all day.

'It will do you good to get out, Miss Reston,' Mrs Wood had remarked pointedly, coming into reception just in time to hear Eve inquiring about a car. 'If you've come for a holiday you won't find much to entertain you inside the hotel, not during the day at any rate. I should drive into the countryside, if I were you, or down to the coast. You'll at least get a change of air.'

Eve had smiled uneasily, conscious of Mrs Wood's close scrutiny, the sudden flicker of speculation in the reception-ist's considering glance. 'I intend to,' she hurriedly assured them both, 'but I have,' she hesitated momentarily before repeating in a nervous rush, 'I have other business to attend to first.'

Swiftly she turned away, in her haste almost snatching the car keys from the desk, anxious to escape the more pertinent questions which she sensed were hovering on the tip of Mrs Wood's tongue. 'I only expect to require a car for one after-noon,' she had murmured before she had fled.

Now, taking a deep breath in an attempt to still the agi-tated tremors that ran through her, Eve advanced a few more steps. There appeared to be no one about, no one to interrupt her first moments of reluctant surveillance as her wide-eyed gaze wandered nervously over a long line of buildings. Slung out, they seemed to be, on a dusty, limitless plain, thrown, as if by some careless artist, across a primeval landscape which stretched between water and sky.

She had only been here three days, but long enough to realise this was a remote land, a land of white horses and herds of cattle, of gipsies and cowboys. The latter she had heard referred to in the hotel as the *gardians* of the Cam-argue. A hard land it seemed to be, although, until now, Eve had liked what little she had seen of it, but there was some-thing about the atmosphere of this ranch which filled her with a peculiar, intangible foreboding.

This house before her was presumably the residence of the DuBares, the place where Céleste DuBare had been born, the home that she had often spoken of with apparent affec-tion at school but which she now seemed to regard rather in

6

the light of a prison—a prison from which she seemed to imagine it was Eve's definite duty to release her!

Beset by numerous anxieties, Eve had allowed that Céleste, in making such assumptions, was probably right, but now she didn't feel so sure? Surely Céleste expected too much? She must have been more than a little crazy to imagine she could bring an almost complete stranger into her family circle and force them to accept her? Already her elder brother, the notorious Raoul DuBare, was hostile, and this before he had even met her. How could Céleste possibly hope that he might react favourably on finding her here, on his very doorstep?

Of course, she hastened to assure herself, it was entirely Raoul DuBare's fault that such a peculiar state of affairs existed. While her eyes remained fixed nervously on the expanse of low stone dwellings, a slightly mutinous change of mood firmed Eve's soft lips with an unfamiliar determination. It was, she considered, entirely because of him that there had been any estrangement between their two families, that he still after all this time appeared to hold her family wholly responsible for the events which had led up to it. To be able to tell him exactly what she thought of his outrageous prejudices had been one of the chief reasons why she had allowed herself to be persuaded to come here. There was a growing urge within herself to meet this man—a man whose forbidding arrogance had been conveyed so realistically both by his actions and in the one letter he had condescended to write to her aunt Mavis, Carol's mother.

It was this thought of her cousin that jerked Eve's mind back to Carol's baby, Michel, who was really the real reason why she had come. Céleste had declared it was her duty.

'Michel is your nephew,' she had said, adding with incredible coolness. 'Now that Carol is dead you have as much right to him as any of us!'

Which wasn't strictly true, as Céleste knew very well. Carol's parents had more or less adopted Eve when she had

7

been eight, after her parents had both lost their lives in an accident. She had been George Reston's brother's child. 'She'll be company for Carol,' he had declared, and his wife had wholeheartedly agreed.

They had been so good to her that Eve had always hoped some day to repay them. Indeed, she had tried to do this almost from the very beginning. She had been a clever child and striving especially to please her aunt and uncle, she had worked hard, eventually delighting them by winning a scholarship to quite a famous girls' school. It had been there that she had met Céleste DuBare, a French girl whose mother had been English, and who still had relations living in Cornwall, not far from Eve's own home.

Céleste, who had only two brothers in France, spent many of her long vacations with these relations, and occasionally she had also stayed with Eve's family. 'My brothers simply consider I am a nuisance,' she had been fond of declaring emphatically. 'They do not care for me.'

Yet, for all her protestations, Céleste's younger brother, Dominique, had visited her regularly at school, and one Sunday Eve had taken them both home for tea. Eve's home, compared with that of Céleste's relations, was extremely modest, but Dominique had apparently found nothing displeasing about it. In fact it seemed that he found something about the small, semi-detached house very pleasing as he returned again and again. But it wasn't until about two years later, when he eloped with Carol, that Eve really understood why he had visited so regularly.

Because they could think of no valid reason for such a furtive marriage, Carol's parents had been upset, but their natural dismay had been nothing compared to Raoul Du-Bare's fury. Over the telephone Mavis had been frozen by his icy disapproval. Céleste's visits had stopped abruptly and she had returned to France straight away. Here, on this very ranch, Raoul DuBare had made things so awkward for Carol that she had begged George and Mavis to wait a while before attempting to come to France.

Raoul had been the reason, Carol had tried to explain after her honeymoon was over, why she and Dominique had been forced to elope. It seemed that Raoul had chosen a French bride for his young brother, and in France, even today, many people still favoured such arrangements. In a way, Carol had generously declared, she quite understood, and time must be allowed for Raoul to forgive and forget. She had begged them to have patience.

But despite Carol's optimism nothing happened, Raoul DuBare being apparently unwilling either to forgive or forget. Carol visited her parents in Cornwall occasionally, but that was all. There was certainly never an invitation for any of them to return with her to the Camargue, a state of affairs which fretted George and Mavis so much they could often talk of little else.

After Carol's baby was born Eve, despite her fondness for them, had felt almost relieved when George, who was a civil engineer, went to Rhodesia, taking Mavis with him. Eve, at that time, had been in London studying to be a children's nannie, the one thing she had been really keen to do, so she couldn't have gone with them even if she had wanted to, but she had fervently hoped the change would do her aunt good and take her mind off Carol for a while.

Yet, unfortunately, George came to blame this very trip for the real tragedy when it struck. Carol, who had not been really well since Michel arrived, had managed to persuade her husband to take her for a short holiday to South Africa to see her parents, against, it was revealed later, Raoul's express wishes. This time it must have seemed to the superstitious that his anger had been justified when the plane carrying Carol and his brother had crashed into the sea with a loss of all life.

The shock had almost proved too much for George, who foolishly blamed himself for the accident. At once, after hearing the news, he had collapsed with a heart attack and been in and out of hospitals ever since. Even now, after almost a year, he was not nearly well enough to travel, and Mavis wrote that his doctor had advised him to remain in Rhodesia, where at least she had plenty of domestic help. She had also, in that last letter, enclosed one which she had received from Raoul DuBare—a letter which had infuriated Eve greatly, and which she still remembered only too clearly.

In it he had assured Mavis, with more than a hint of cruelty, that he was more than able to take care of Carol's baby himself, and it would be better for all concerned if they continued to go their separate ways.

'A veritable tug of war would do the child no good,' he had said, 'and considering your husband's state of health no one would look on him as a suitable guardian. In my care he will want for nothing and have a better life than you could ever hope to provide, providing, of course, you do not seek to interfere . . .'

His last sentence had seemed to hold more than a measure of insidious warning. Stay away, it had implied, or else! And, at that particular time, there had seemed little else that any of them could do but to comply with Raoul DuBare's wishes. But inside Eve was still a smouldering anger, over a year later still as fresh as when she had first read his letter with its intimidating, forceful handwriting. One day, she had vowed, she would surely find a means of hurting him as badly as he had wounded her aunt and uncle, and poor Carol, whom he had scarcely ever allowed them to see!

Once her training had been completed, Eve had taken a temporary job in London, looking after the small son of a French business man and his wife. Carefully, she had saved her salary, hoping, when her job was finished, to be able to fly to South Africa to see George and Mavis, but before this could happen, to her surprise, letters began to arrive in a positive deluge from Céleste.

Eve had seen nothing of Céleste since she had left school, and now she wrote: 'I wish to live in Paris. It was all practically arranged before the accident. After that, Raoul declared my duty was here, at the ranch. I must remain to look after Michel who, even now, is still a baby. Raoul appears to think I must share the responsibility of seeing he is reared correctly, and seems to take it for granted that I should willingly sacrifice the best years of my life. Our cousin Nadine assures me I am wasted here in the Camargue, and, while she is not nearly so strict as Raoul, would look after me well. Raoul appears to imagine I should be content with the Rallye and a few carefully chosen friends!'

The Rallye, Eve knew vaguely, was a sort of private group, formed by the mothers of the upper classes who regularly gave dances so that their daughters might meet only eligible young people. Eve's employers had mentioned it and Céleste had talked of it at school, but as Eve had never moved in such circles herself she had paid little attention.

It had been Céleste's next words which had utterly dismayed her. 'You must come, Eve, and help me talk to Raoul. If I do have some responsibility regarding Michel, then so do you, and you must share it. You are his aunt, exactly as I am . . .'

After numerous attempts, Eve had replied as best she could, pointing out bluntly in the end that, as Céleste must know very well, she had merely been Carol's cousin, so wasn't really Michel's aunt, and consequently would only be wasting her time. Raoul would never be prepared to receive her.

Back had come Céleste's next letter—furiously! 'You must come! If you continue to refuse I will bring Michel immediately to England. Then the fire will be in the fat—or how is it you say! I will swear you invited me and Raoul will believe me. He will accuse you of persuasion and he will be very, very angry, and you do not know what my brother is like when he is angry, *ma chérie*!'

Recalling all she knew of him, Eve had no real doubts about Raoul DuBare's temper. Unconsciously she had shivered. It was as if the dark personality of the man had even then reached out and touched her.

Céleste had finished on a pleading note. 'But you know I will only do this if all else fails. I beg of you to reconsider, *chérie*. Raoul is a man of many moods, if you caught him in a good one he might listen to you. You are almost twenty-two, more than a year older than me, and most attractive with your lint-fair hair and wide eyes. It is when you smile that I think Raoul will see in them that which he likes in a woman. So you must smile, Eve, and assure him times are changing and girls are not to be kept in absolute seclusion any more, that you are quite prepared to look after Michel for a few months while I enjoy a little freedom. After all, I cannot see how he can remain so rigid when he is so fond of his own amours! I know of more than one *mademoiselle— madame . . .*'

Céleste had rambled on so much in this vein that Eve had grown alarmed. She had no wish to hear about Raoul Du-Bare's indiscretions, as she already despised him, but Céleste's obviously unbalanced attitude regarding her immediate problems filled Eve with apprehension. She might indeed be quite capable of arriving in London as she threatened!

And for all her resolve not to set even one foot on French soil, Eve's mind had clung uneasily to the problem of Michel. Was it desirable that a young baby should be reared by such people? Yet might it not be worse for him to live in possibly inferior digs in London—always supposing the arrogant Raoul allowed him to remain! Yet it wasn't until the third letter, when Céleste threatened to contact George and Mavis, that Eve felt left with no other alternative but to give in. Clearly, if faced with even an inkling of such a dilemma, George might again collapse, and Eve knew it was up to her to rule out the possibility of any such thing happening.

By return she had promised cautiously that she would pay a short visit, and immediately Céleste, as if anticipating her surrender, had sent a list of instructions. There was a hotel, a short distance from Les Saintes Maries, run by an English-woman who had always rooms to spare at the beginning of the season. It was an ideal place for Eve to stay. It had the decided advantage of being both convenient and several miles from Céleste's home. Eve was to go there and Céleste would get in touch as soon as she arrived. On no account was Eve to try and contact her.

In spite of being inwardly almost terrified of such an undertaking, Eve had also felt an undeniable flicker of tense excitement. Previously she had had neither the time nor money for foreign travel—now she must find both, yet the prospect, while daunting, was not, she soon realised, insurmountable. Her recent job completed, she took a little of the money she had saved to buy material for dresses which she made quickly herself, then positively clutching her passport and a few small pieces of luggage, one spring evening she had caught a train from Victoria to Dover, then on to Calais, arriving several hours later in Paris. From there the remainder of her journey south had proved much easier than she had expected, and would have been, had she not had so much on her mind, very enjoyable.

The hotel she had found without much difficulty, although, contrary to what Céleste had told her, almost all the rooms had been taken and, but for the intervention of Mrs Wood, the proprietress, Eve fancied she might have been turned away. Taking compassion, it seemed, on Eve's rather panic-stricken face she had assured her she could have a room for at least a few days. Eve had thanked her gratefully, adding that she didn't expect to require it for longer than this as when it became convenient she was to stay with a friend.

But for three whole days Eve had waited in vain for Céleste. Strung up to a high degree of tenseness, she had scarcely dared leave her room for fear she should miss the girl should she telephone or arrive. On the fourth morning, beset by a wholly frightening despair, Eve rang the ranch in the vague hope that Céleste might answer. It was a risk she had felt driven to take. At first she had thought it was

Céleste who answered, but when Eve spoke her name there had been only a short, sharp silence before a stranger, another woman, had informed her that Mademoiselle Céleste was not there.

Filled with alarm, Eve had quickly dropped the receiver. Where Céleste was she had no idea, but she was strongly convinced that something must have happened. There and then Eve decided she would no longer remain hiding in the hotel like some errant criminal or defenceless animal. She must go out to the ranch immediately and get this thing settled once and for all. Céleste obviously didn't intend to get in touch as she had promised, and, at that moment, Eve felt suddenly too incensed to even consider returning home without seeing somebody—even if that somebody had to be Raoul DuBare himself. He might be a force to be reckoned with, but so could she be on occasion, and he couldn't possibly eat her.

Without giving herself a chance to calm down, when it might have been possible she would have changed her mind, she had started out in one of Mrs Wood's cars, and now that she had actually found her way to the ranch, the only hurdle left seemed that of having to knock on the door. Which proved the worst of the lot, now that her defiant temper had subsided a little.

The house looked shabbier than she had imagined it would be, a great barn of a place with solid stone walls and a heavy roof of straw beneath which small windows peered curiously. There was an overall shabbiness which Eve found in no way compatible with the DuBare image. Maybe Raoul DuBare spent his reputed wealth on other things?

Whipping up her already failing courage, she knocked louder than she might have done in other circumstances, and heard her thunderous rapping echoing inside, hollowly, as though the place was empty. She was startled by such a thought as she waited. Céleste must surely be around somewhere, especially when she was being forced to look after

Michel? But when eventually the door did open, Eve found herself staring into the eyes of a stout, elderly woman—a woman who was definitely not Céleste!

If Eve was curiously bereft of speech the person in front of her was not. Swiftly she drew herself up, her black eyes darting over Eve's slight figure as if actively resenting such an intrusion. '*Que voulez-vous?* What do you want, *mademoiselle?*' she repeated, as Eve didn't immediately reply.

Quickly Eve tried to pull herself together, gulping on a deep breath. '*Je regrette . . .*' she found herself apologising politely, trying to subdue a sharp resentment at the woman's tone. 'May I come in?' she requested abruptly, 'I have called to see Mademoiselle Céleste. I am a friend of hers.' Cautiously, and only just in time, Eve withheld her own name. Perhaps, in remaining anonymous, she would stand a better chance of seeing Céleste.

The woman continued to stare suspiciously, her doubts not wholly alleviated, it seemed, by Eve's very good French. 'You are not one of us, *mademoiselle*,' she said at last. 'We do not care for strangers here.'

'But you are mistaken, *madame*,' Eve cried, losing some discretion in a moment when she felt the door about to be slammed in her face. 'I cannot explain to you, but if you would please tell Miss Céleste I am here I can assure you all will be well.'

'*Mademoiselle*—I——' the woman was clearly still far from convinced as she blinked uncertainly.

Attempting, in a moment of insanity, to push an advantage she obviously didn't have, Eve interrupted wildly. 'I should like, if Miss Céleste is not here, to see the baby.'

'*L'enfant?*' Pinched lips pursed with disapproval in flabby cheeks, as for a startled instant the woman dropped her guard, allowing Eve to push past her into the house.

'Yes, the *enfant* Michel.' Following up the move which appeared to make her position stronger, Eve spoke firmly. 'I should like to see him at once. *Vous comprenez?*'

As the woman shook her head in a dumbfounded fashion, Eve felt instinctively she had made a mistake. Yet it would be impossible to try and change matters now. Besides, her head was so tense with nerves that anything she might say could only make matters worse, and she had no possible excuse for thrusting her way in here uninvited. '*Je regrette* ...' she apologised again, distractedly, as the woman turned away.

If Eve had suspected she was about to be thrown out she was wholly relieved when, as if completely nonplussed, the woman muttered sullenly. 'If you will wait here, *mademoiselle*, I will see what I can do.'

Left on her own, new fears seemed to rush upon Eve from seemingly many directions. The whole thing, the very atmosphere of the place, her own stupidity in coming here, was frightening. Helplessly she gazed about her. It wasn't the sort of dwelling she had ever associated with Céleste Du-Bare, nor could she remember Carol describing her home in France like this, although she had always been reluctant to talk of it. The house was unusual, different from any farmhouse Eve had seen in England. A flight of stone steps led up to the first storey, where the family obviously lived. These ended on a sort of terrace and a door opened straight into the kitchen. This was a very large room, furnished with a long wooden table, flanked by benches and wood-seated chairs. There was a fire smouldering on a flat hearthstone in spite of the heat of the day, and from the chimney hung chains on which a large pot was suspended over the flames. The strong, appetising aroma suggested soup might be cooking. There were also, Eve noticed, inglenook benches on either side of the wide chimney, and while the whole conveyed an impression of rough comfort it seemed scarcely in keeping with the rich bourgeois.

Eve sighed, suddenly weary; this was a minor consideration. She was, after all, only in the kitchen, a room which the DuBares probably never came near. Where on earth was Céleste? The woman had been long gone. Renewed indignation flooded through her so that when the door behind her was rudely flung open she swung swiftly around, her face taut with a nervous anger.

But again it wasn't Céleste. It was a man who stood there regarding her from peculiarly light green eyes. Eve didn't think she had ever seen anyone like him! It wasn't that he seemed to loom over her, his expression hard and indifferent, seemingly as annoyed as her own ... It was perhaps more in the way he stood, impassively, something that combined with the darkness of him and the clothes he wore. Startled, Eve's eyes took in the high-heeled leather boots, his wide-brimmed hat, so reminiscent of a western cowboys. As he drew nearer her nostrils were assailed by the smell of warm leather and sweat and she flinched, as if instinctively defensive against the lightning effect the man had on her. Though obviously almost covered in dust his good looks were undeniable, yet because of the dust which seemed to cling to every determined groove of his body, Eve would have been hard put to even guess at his age. A lot older than herself, she thought, well into his thirties. Her heart lurched as she returned his narrowed, inquiring glance, feeling suddenly the impact of an intently sharpening gaze. And she didn't, not after those first few wholly depressing moments, need to be told exactly who he was.

Yet it was he who spoke first as his eyes ran coolly appraising down the whole slim length of her. 'Good afternoon, *mademoiselle*,' he said, his voice curiously stirring her already heightened senses. 'What can I do for you? You are inquiring about my nephew, I am told?'

'Yes—yes, I am.' In her confusion Eve omitted to return his greeting, or indeed to speak French. Before his intense masculinity her own gaze faltered and fell as wildly she tried to decide what she must do. Hadn't she promised Céleste she would not betray her? She drew a quick breath without realising it was quite audible. How foolish she had been to come to the ranch this morning! How could she have imagined there would be little risk of running into Raoul DuBare? He had probably known the very minute she had approached his land.

'I'm Eve Reston,' she went on in a breathless rush. 'My cousin Carol was married to your brother. She used to live here ...' With some dismay Eve halted, realising she was giving needless explanations in a muddled fashion that would never impress the man before her. 'You see, I know who you are,' she managed to whisper, as Raoul DuBare stiffened.

His eyes, icy with anger, flicked her flushed cheeks, but there was no indication that her news startled him. Coldly sardonic, his fine sarcasm like a douche of cold water, he inclined his head. '*Mademoiselle*,' he said, smoothly, 'I suggest you go no further, you would merely be wasting your breath. Such information as you have given is not impossible to find. Have you any proof of your identity?'

Eve's eyes flew to his blankly, already hating him. It seemed a twist of fate that she carried nothing with her; she didn't even have her handbag in the car, unfortunately having left it lying on the reception desk at the hotel. She had, in fact, become aware of this before she had gone very far and had almost gone back, then decided this would be silly as the receptionist must have noticed and it would be well taken care of until she returned. Did Raoul DuBare actually think she was an impostor, or was he simply seeking an excuse to get rid of her? What reason would she have for pretending to be someone she was not? 'This is ridiculous,' she said breathlessly, attempting to ignore his query, to treat it with the contempt she was sure it deserved.

His eyes glinted. He was not to be put off so easily. 'You must carry something on your person?'

'No,' the turmoil within her tightened her throat painfully. 'But I am not a liar, *monsieur*, I do know your sister.'

'So you would like me to think.' He was looking straight at her, his gaze derisive. 'Other would-be kidnappers have sought to convince me of the same thing.'

'Kidnappers?' Eve's mind felt curiously disconnected with shock, and she was unable to turn away from the brilliance of those strange eyes. For a moment her voice seemed lost in her throat and she couldn't utter another word. Surely she couldn't have heard properly?

As if he read her mind with a devilish accuracy, his mouth hardened. 'You heard correctly, *mademoiselle*, and I might add that the ingeniousness of criminals never ceases to amaze me. One would never imagine they would employ a girl with a face as deceptively innocent as yours. How did you get here?'

The abruptness of this last question cut like a scalpel through Eve's last remaining fragments of evasion. 'By car,' she confessed weakly.

'By car? I do not see any such vehicle. Where is it?'

'Oh . . .' Swamped suddenly by a cold apprehension, Eve stared at him aghast. 'It's—I mean . . .'

'Yes——?' he chopped through the mumbled words sharply, malice in every hard line of him.

Eve caught her breath at his tone, yet was impelled by it to continue more clearly, 'I left it a little way down the road, behind a clump of trees.'

'Hidden!' Now she could see triumph shooting almost visibly through him, but it was too late to regret she hadn't driven boldly up to the front door.

'It was because I was nervous!' There was a feeling she was caught somewhere in the middle of a nightmare, and only able to find answers which seemed to give the opposite impression to that which she sought.

'Or afraid of being caught?' he taunted, without giving her a chance to be more explicit, his own opinion obviously all he was prepared to believe. 'You were apparently prepared for the necessity to escape quickly should the need arise. And your fears were no doubt justified, *mademoiselle*. Men frequently overlook the fact that a woman's nerve is not all it should be, and they very rarely possess the expertise to prove satisfactory accomplices in a scheme such as this. Your friends should also have considered that Raoul DuBare might know too much about women ever to be fooled by any one of them.'

Eve spun on him in a fury, goaded beyond measure by his outrageous line of attack. So he knew all there was to know about women! She could quite believe he thought he did, but his mouth had too cruel a twist ever to have known tenderness. His affairs, she guessed instinctively, would be violent, in keeping with the terrain he lived in, subtly calculated to bring pleasure only to himself. A woman's feelings would be of minor consideration so far as this man was concerned. Convulsively Eve found herself shuddering as her wide-eyed glance clung to his hard features, not knowing quite where such intimate thoughts had come from, but willing to be convinced that they had been wholly prompted by his vicious, unfounded suspicions regarding her integrity. Small wonder Carol hadn't liked him!

Dazed, she passed a numbed hand across her gently perspiring forehead, trying to collect her scattered thoughts into some semblance of order. If, as he arrogantly declared, he knew everything about women, then he might easily have guessed how very little she knew about men. He was a stranger, an unknown quantity, whom a girl with so little experience would be crazy to tangle with. No doubt, if he chose, he could be as ruthless as this harsh, barren land. Yet how could she let his terrible accusations pass as though she had never heard him? Human nature was surely never meant to be as tolerant as all that!

'Monsieur DuBare,' she found herself saying, coldly, 'you simply can't realise the seriousness of your stupid allegations?'

The word stupid must have been a mistake, as immediately she had uttered it his jaw tightened savagely and he replied in a hard, tight voice, in no way inclined it seemed to take back a single sentence of what he had said. Indeed he went on, intent obviously to insult further. 'Your friends have certainly slipped up this time, *mademoiselle*. You are too naïve to fool anyone!'

'Why, how dare you!' Eve felt herself quiver in an agony of futility. 'I only wanted to see Carol's baby. Why should I want to kidnap him?'

His eyes went almost insultingly over her, in a way calculated to make her blood pressure soar. He laughed, but completely without humour, his lips curling contemptuously. 'Money can tempt even the best of us, *mademoiselle*, but for those of low principles it can prove irresistible. A god—a factor to rule one's life.'

Stung beyond measure, Eve cried recklessly, 'What money could I expect to receive from you, *monsieur*?' Deliberately she forced her eyes to travel around the shabby living room before coming back to linger on his dusty faded shirt, a button of which was torn off at the neck to expose an expanse of brown skin. Yet to become suddenly conscious of all that bare skin, covered as it was by rough dark hairs, was more than she had bargained for, and her heart lurched in a frightening manner. She felt hot, breathless, incredibly nervy, as his strength seemed to hit her like a physical force, warning her that whatever else this man might be he was no weakling. Lowering her startled gaze quickly before it could betray her, she added sharply, 'From the style of your house it's obvious you are no millionaire!'

He took a threatening step towards her, his hand reaching out to grasp her arm, his face hard with anger, as if her imprudent observation had proved the final straw. '*Mon dieu!*' he exclaimed, 'one can at least admire a thief who acknowledges the blackness of his heart, but for one who pleads perpetually of innocence I have nothing but contempt.'

Her face white, Eve tried to free her arm, but his fingers held, gripping with the remorseless cruelty of steel, and the taunting ring of his words seemed to explode in her ears. 'Good heavens,' she choked, 'Michel can scarcely be safe with a man like you!'

His breath was warm on her cold skin as he brought his face oppressively within inches of her own. 'I don't know quite what you refer to, *mademoiselle*, but I am asking you to leave before I lose both my patience and my temper completely. Then you might not escape so easily,' he threatened.

'And if I refuse?' Above the clamorous beating of her heart which seemed to shake her slender body, Eve attempted defiantly to ignore his threatening tones. The only thing to do, she was convinced, was to stand her ground. This man would be too used to having his own way to appreciate grovelling in others. 'You can't force me to leave,' she challenged unwisely, as if discrediting his ability to do so.

His white teeth snapped together as he regarded her with black cynicism. 'There you are mistaken, *mademoiselle*. I am more than capable of removing anyone from my premises. Perhaps you would care for a demonstration?'

To Eve's horror, before she quite understood his intentions, his grasp on her arm tightened, his other arm going hard around her as he almost carried her from the room. Ruthlessly he held her to him, taking her swiftly down the uneven steps that led to the ground, taking no notice whatsoever of her frantic struggles as he deposited her roughly on to the baked earth below. The totally uncaring thrust he administered as he released her caused her to lose what little balance she had left and land in an undignified heap at his feet. Into her dazed ears, a moment later, came the sound of the door slamming decisively—a crash which informed her indisputably that he had not even waited to see if she could pick herself up!

CHAPTER TWO

ALMOST crying with fright, Eve scrambled to her feet, only half aware of her torn dress and bruised limbs. Wishing fervently that she had been a man, able to rush after Raoul DuBare and punish him for his sins, she stared for a long painful minute at the stone steps up which he had disappeared, obviously quite satisfied that he was rid of his unwelcome guest.

A whimpering sob catching in her throat, Eve turned away, her temper deserting her as quickly as it had risen. Left in her heart was only an aching despair, a sense of frustration, a guilty conviction that much of what had happened might have been her own fault. That she must have managed Raoul DuBare badly for him to turn her out like this?

Yet her own fault or not she had never felt so horribly treated! Raoul DuBare was a positive monster, a brute, and she regretted that she had no means of conveying to him clearly exactly what she thought of his diabolical behaviour. But then he would only laugh. She could imagine that strong dark head thrown back, his wicked eyes gleaming, and the picture thus conjured up disturbed so strangely that she immediately put it from her.

Biting sharply her full lower lip as her side hurt, Eve walked slowly back to the car, determined not to obey an urgent inclination to run. She wouldn't put it past the man to be still standing by the window, making sure she went. Her chin tilted, she tried to move steadily. She must show him she was not completely defeated—if he was really watching, which, casting foolish fancies aside, she very much doubted.

Inside the car it was hot, suffocatingly so, as she hadn't remembered to lower the window when she had left it. The seats burnt and she winced convulsively as tears of self-pity began to run helplessly down her flushed cheeks. She knew a terrible feeling of being totally alone and deserted, and an equally intense if irrational longing for the comfort of a loving breast to weep on. Attempting to pull herself together, she groped for a handkerchief, the only likely means, she told herself wryly, she might ever have of drying her tears. And if she was to return the hired car by lunch time she must get back to the hotel.

Turning quickly on the hardened track, she pressed her foot to the accelerator, heedless of the ensuing dust as she left the ranch far behind. A wind blew in a tormented fashion over the land and Eve didn't care for it. It was the mistral, and she had learnt that with the exception of the summer months, there were very few days in the Camargue without it. Today it blew strongly, buffeting the small car, whirling the inevitable dust clouds across the horizon. There were other minor hazards, apparently, if in a more enticing form. Freshwater marshes, grown densely with reeds, a trap for the unwary. Or the more attractive but brackish lakes, *étangs*, where other dangers might lurk, but none of these, she decided miserably, could be worse than the human element, in the form of Raoul DuBare!

Try as she might to distract it, Eve's mind kept tenaciously returning to him—and Céleste. She had come especially to see Céleste and failed, and there seemed little more she could do about it. It was no use arguing with herself that she might have tried harder. If she went on like this she would only make herself ill. With a little effort she might even convince herself that Raoul might have been more successfully approached another way, but no matter how they had met such a meeting would have been doomed to failure.

Straight away she had sensed in him an antagonism which had not been wholly because of baby Michel. Eve's painful sigh of bewilderment was constricted. Babies such as

Michel, from ordinary families, were surely in no great danger of being kidnapped? Raoul DuBare, in accusing her as he had, must be more than a little crazy!

Back at the hotel, Eve left the car keys in reception, and thankfully retrieved her bag before retiring to her room. Once there she sank down on to the edge of her bed trying to review the situation clearly. The morning had proved a complete failure, in the nature of a disaster, but something else disturbed her almost as much. Her money was running out. Gloomily she surveyed the contents of her handbag. There was only enough left to see her through another day or two, and then only if she economised on meals. A frown of apprehension creased her smooth brow as she counted her remaining francs. It had perhaps been foolish to come with so little, but it was all she had decided she could spare from the money she had set aside to go to South Africa, and Céleste had promised she wouldn't have to stay at the hotel for more than two nights.

However—Eve closed her bag sharply; it was no good crying over spilt milk. She had done enough of that already. She must arrange to leave tomorrow. This would at least give her a few more hours to think of a way by which she might still see Carol's baby. If it was at all possible?

Eve's head, as she sat there, began to ache, and the longer she thought about it the more confused she became. To her shame all she could visualise was not the baby, but a man's hard face, a proud, dark profile, the quivering reaction of her own traitorous body to the hurting strength of his arms. She merely had to close her eyes to hear the attractive vibrance of his voice which had seemed to strike some answering chord within herself, making contact as it had seemed to with every sensitive nerve. She would do better, she knew, to remember that his voice had had a volume of bitterness in it, and that his eyes had held cold cynicism, all too clearly reflecting his opinion of women on the whole. And the utter indignity of that last scene!

It wasn't until she was about to tidy herself before going

25

out to find a cheap snack rather than indulge in an expensive lunch that the idea came. Not a very original one, or exciting, but because the arid regions of her mind seemed incapable of producing another, she snatched at it. She might find herself a job.

Desperately she tried to think if there was a French equivalent of the English employment bureau and failed. Again a frown drew her feathery brows together doubtfully. How did one set about getting work in a foreign land? She couldn't remember whether she would require a work permit or not. Some regulations, she knew, had been changed. Maybe the best thing she could do was to ask Mrs Wood, who seemed always so willing to advise her guests. Quickly, without stopping to change her soiled dress, Eve rinsed her hands and rushed downstairs.

It was almost three o'clock and the hotel was quiet, many of the visitors being down on the nearest beach or gently snoozing beneath mammoth umbrellas on the hotel lawns. Mrs Wood was in her office as Eve hoped she would be. There was no one else around apart from her secretary whom she dismissed to reception when Eve asked tentatively if she could have a private word with her.

'Now, my dear,' she said briskly, as the door closed behind the girl, 'what can I do for you? Sit down.'

Eve hesitated, her face suddenly pale, scarcely aware of being watched closely as she took the chair Mrs Wood indicated. 'I'm sorry,' she began in some confusion, with an apologetic glance after the disappearing secretary, 'I really didn't mean to interrupt you like this.' She continued in a rush when Mrs Wood told her not to worry, 'The thing is, Mrs Wood, my affairs here haven't worked out quite as I expected, and I should like to find a job. It's just that I don't really know where to start and wondered if you could help me?'

If Mrs Wood was surprised she didn't show it, although she didn't reply immediately. But her sparse lashes flickered as her glance rested curiously on Eve's slightly torn dress, and her eyes narrowed a fraction. 'I rather got the impression,' she said, 'that you were here to meet a friend, a boy-friend, perhaps. Someone who's let you down?'

Eve flushed, momentarily startled, in no way prepared for such an unexpected contingency, though, regarding her present position introspectively, who was she to quibble? Wasn't she in an extremely awkward position? False pride could have no place in her life at the moment. Yet, it came to her instinctively, because the DuBares were involved she must be cautious. The Woods had been in the district five years, they must know the DuBares or, at least, of them. It might not do to be too indiscreet in that direction. So ignoring a natural desire to confess the truth, she managed to merely nod her head evasively, hoping that Mrs Wood would probe no further.

Mrs Wood didn't. Eve's pink cheeks and hastily lowered lashed convinced Mrs Wood that her guess had been accurate, and she was too busy to waste more time. 'I'm sorry, my dear,' she said, 'but these things do happen. And now you would like to stay a little longer, in the hope perhaps that you might be eventually reunited with this young man? Well, you say you would like work, but are you trained for anything, dear?'

Quick relief overcoming a faintly indignant, if ridiculous tremor at Mrs Wood's swift disposal of her affairs, Eve found herself agreeing almost eagerly and acquainting Mrs Wood with a few details of her training. Whatever else she was prepared for it hadn't been Mrs Wood's delighted exclamation.

'Why, you might indeed be the answer to my prayers!' the woman smiled, her gaze resting with renewed interest on Eve's face. 'I usually employ a nurse, you see, as many of my guests have children and they welcome someone who will take them off their hands occasionally and keep an eye on them in the evening when they're out, or even simply dining in the hotel. Unfortunately the woman I've employed for the past two years has been called urgently back to England as her mother is very ill, and I'm actually looking for someone suitable to take her place. She hopes to return in a week or two, and, as she's so good, I promised to keep her job open for her, for at least a while, but if you would care to have it on a short term basis, then it's yours.'

Minutes later, as she almost flew back to her room, Eve found it difficult to believe it had all happened. With an efficiency which Eve had found rather frightening, Mrs Wood had completed a few details, her brisk businesslike manner proving instantly why her hotel was such a success. She was delighted, she said, with Eve's qualifications, her satisfaction being obvious when she learnt that, as well as French, Eve also had a passable fluency in German and Italian, languages having been one of her favourite subjects at school.

'As we get quite a lot of visitors from these two countries,' Mrs Wood explained, 'this will be useful.' She had dismissed Eve then, after telling her she could start right away, the sooner the better.

Eve had agreed, very willingly, promising to begin that very evening, without completely realising exactly what she was taking on.

During the days that followed, however, reality caught up and a little of her new optimism faded as she found herself having to take sole charge of numerous small children. There seemed little consolation in reminding herself that she was still in the Camargue, and because of Raoul DuBare's attitude had not been forced to return home immediately, without any hope of ever seeing Michel again.

Her new job Eve found interesting but very hard work, which wasn't, when she stopped to think, very surprising, as the hotel was a large one and most of the guests appeared to have their families with them. Sometimes she found it difficult to make up her mind who was the most demanding, the children or their parents. The latter apparently expected her to fetch and carry for them long after their offspring were in bed. Comparing this with her first position in London, Eve realised that there she had had very little to do. Yet here she had too much, and her gratitude towards Mrs Wood changed rapidly to a rather wry cynicism, which fortunately she managed to keep to herself. It could, she was aware, prove a blessing in disguise that she was left with little time to brood over the DuBares, being usually too exhausted to spare them more than the occasional passing thought. If she did get round to thinking of them her mind, too tired by the chatter of small, excited tongues, refused to come up with anything new. On her day off, she resolved, she must try to get out and explore the area, then the answer might present itself as to what she must do.

It was on the following Tuesday morning, just before she was about to take a group of small children to play in the paddling pool, that she received another shock. She had gone with a parent to collect an inflatable ring from a car and was on her way back alone when to her utter amazement Céleste drew up. She was driving a small, bright yellow car and, although Eve could only stand and stare at her speechlessly, Céleste didn't seem in any way abnormally affected by the sight of Eve, her only concession to bewilderment being in the glance she directed at the collection of toys clutched in Eve's hands.

'Hello, *chérie*!' she laughed, her eyes crinkling with a sudden merriment as she wound down her car window and leaned out. 'Don't tell me you intend all those for Michel? He is not yet of an age, *chérie*, and he has enough.'

'For Michel?' Indignantly Eve stopped in her tracks, her own glance widening. Really, for sheer arrogance these DuBares took a lot of beating! Here she was, almost exhausted after a week of worry, not to mention work, and all Céleste could do, after keeping her in suspense all this time, was to giggle and pass some ridiculous remark. 'Really,

Céleste,' she managed at last with uncontrollable bluntness, 'you do have a nerve!'

'Why, how do you mean?' the girl inquired absently, to Eve's disgust not even yet displaying a hint of remorse as, after her first few flippant words of greeting, she chose to glance about the car park furtively as if scared someone would see her.

'Look, Eve,' she rushed on nervously, not waiting for Eve to answer, 'I think it would be better if we talked somewhere else. I don't wish the so busy Mrs Wood to see us together. She has the ear of my brother, that one.'

'It was your idea that I stayed here in the first place,' Eve reminded her, resentful that Céleste was avoiding the fact that she was a week late, that no apology was forthcoming. 'And the so busy Mrs Wood, as you call her, happens to be my employer, so I can't do what you ask even if I wanted to.'

'Eve!' For the first time Céleste seemed to look at her properly. 'But what is the matter, *chérie*? You act strangely —and what do you mean. How can Mrs Wood be your employer? *Je ne comprends pas*—I don't understand.'

Coldly Eve stared at her. 'You appear to forget that I've been here over a week. I had to do something when you didn't turn up.'

'A week!' Céleste threw up her hands, her little squeal of dismay very French. 'But, darling, you distinctly stated you would arrive today!'

'I said the first of the month.'

'No, Eve, you said the ninth!'

'Listen,' Eve began fiercely, 'I made a special note of the date, the day and everything. I couldn't possibly afford to make such a mistake. Have you my letter?'

'I'm sorry, *chérie*.' For the first time Céleste had the grace to look slightly ashamed. 'You see, Raoul came across me reading it just after the post had been. I was forced quickly to put it in the fire and immediately he imagines it is from my boy-friend whom he does not care for. But I could swear you said the ninth.'

Eve sighed deeply, restraining her growing impatience, fully aware that so far as this went Céleste was quite probably speaking the truth. In the best of circumstances she had never been able to memorise properly, but Eve couldn't understand why she hadn't, in this one instance, been particularly careful. Or was it that Raoul DuBare struck the same fear into those he loved as he did strangers? Remembering his cold light eyes, Eve found no difficulty in believing it.

'I came last week,' she repeated in a more even tone, feeling it pointless to argue further. 'I waited for three whole days before going out to the ranch.'

'You came to the ranch?' Céleste's eyes were like startled saucers, and for a moment she seemed to forget the need to leave the hotel quickly as she gazed incredulously at Eve's taut face.

In a stony voice Eve replied, 'Yes—and your brother threw me out, literally! But I didn't see you.'

'Mon dieu!' Céleste's exclamation was a hoarse whisper. 'You must have been crazy ever to contemplate such a thing! I have warned you before about Raoul. And to arrive at the ranch, just like that. You are an imbécile! What day was this, you say?'

'Wednesday...' beneath such an onslaught, Eve's pale cheeks flushed with anger.

'Wednesday—mercredi? How was it I did not see you? I was at home all day. And how do you mean, he threw you out?'

'You don't have to disturb yourself,' Eve assured her bitterly. 'It hurt, but then I suppose you're quite used to seeing visitors treated in this fashion.'

'But I'm not! I can't think how ... Look, Eve,' Céleste, a frantic frown on her narrow brows, glanced about wildly. 'Look, darling, we can't talk here. Mrs Wood does know

31

Raoul, occasionally she hires our horses, and she is always relating, or trying to relate, some little tittle-tattle. Raoul does his best to avoid her, of course, but it is not always possible. She has the determination, you see, and Raoul is a man women like. I'm sorry everything has been—what do you call it—mixed up, but if the fault was mine, and I suppose it will be, then you must forgive me. But you must also agree to meet me somewhere and discuss what is to happen next.'

'But your brother?'

'Oh, if only you had waited!' Céleste gave a despairing little moan. 'Now Raoul is upset and everything will take much longer to sort out. We must reach a solution, but not here. You must come with me at once.'

Such audacity! Eve shrugged indifferently, not in any way impressed. With that hint of imperviousness as she spoke, Céleste reminded her too forcibly of her brother, and a violent dislike of Raoul DuBare restrained her from agreeing too readily with Céleste's suggestion that she should go with her now. Besides, she couldn't just walk out. She wasn't free to do so. Mrs Wood might have her faults, but she had provided a job when Eve had been desperate and Eve had no intention of letting her down.

'I can't possibly get away,' she told an agitated Céleste. 'You must wait until I get time off, and, as I've only just started, I don't know when that will be.'

'But you are entitled to time off, *chérie*.' Taking not the slightest notice of Eve's protests, Céleste named a small village some distance away along the coast. 'I shall meet you there tomorrow. This will enable you to make the necessary arrangements.'

'I don't know.' Illogically Eve began to reconsider, wavering in spite of herself. 'Mrs Wood does appear to imagine I've had words with a boy-friend, and I didn't exactly correct the impression.'

To her surprise, Céleste's gay laughter pealed out. 'Oh,

Eve,' she cried, 'Raoul would be flattered!' Then, just as swiftly as she smiled she frowned, as something suddenly occurred to her. 'If Raoul threw you out, it was surely not because he knew who you are? You can't possibly have told him!'

Again Eve felt her cheeks go red, and hated herself for feeling guilty. 'I suppose I did in a way,' she heard herself admitting reluctantly, 'but I'm not certain he quite realised. He seemed to imagine I was there at the instigation of a gang, all set to kidnap Michel. This, I gathered, was what infuriated him.'

'Kidnap Michel—you!' Céleste stared at Eve disbelievingly. 'But yes,' she added mysteriously, 'I do see. We did have a little trouble, but, so far as you are concerned, it still doesn't make sense.'

'What do you mean?' Eve asked jerkily, glancing swiftly at her watch. The children would be tired of waiting.

'I'm sorry, Eve, I can't explain now. There is no time.' From the corner of her eye Céleste caught a glimpse of Mrs Wood's searching figure. 'Here comes your so good employer, no doubt wondering if someone has kidnapped her new slave. Meet me tomorrow at three, *chérie*. You must!'

Flooded with a kind of angry frustration, her cry of protest lost beneath the noise of an over accelerated engine, Eve watched as Céleste swung the small car swiftly around and disappeared, thus avoiding a curious Mrs Wood. That she had left without offering even one constructive suggestion filled Eve with despair.

It was with some reluctance that she did eventually ask for a few hours off next day, pretending not to notice Mrs Wood's disapproving expression as she agreed. Eve was quickly learning that there was a great deal of difference between being a hotel guest and an employee. Her room had immediately been changed, the one she occupied now little more than a cubbyhole with one tiny window half way up the wall, which opened only with the exertion of a great deal of pressure. Her meals, naturally, were not the same, nor had she expected them to be, but the size of the portions were often so meagre that she frequently felt hungry, even though her appetite was normally small.

'It is just her way.' Other members of the staff shrugged off Mrs Wood's meanness indifferently. 'In some things Madame is generous—in others, just the opposite. It can be better to eat outside, or take extra food to one's room.'

But this cost money, Eve knew, and she still didn't seem to have enough to spare. Resigned, she remained silent.

During the next weeks she managed to meet Céleste occasionally. The other nanny whom Mrs Wood employed didn't return and Eve decided to stay on at the hotel a little longer, at least until she had seen Michel. She thought it advisable to write to Rhodesia and explain where she was, though she skipped several details, and when Mavis replied, full of gratitude, asking eagerly about her grandson, Eve felt forced to renew her determination to see him, despite Raoul DuBare's attitude.

The first time she met Céleste they talked, among other things, about Michel, Céleste endeavouring to explain how he had almost been kidnapped.

'It was while Carol was out shopping in town. I was with her. A woman managed somehow to get into the house and Marie, our maid, actually caught her carrying Michel out. She said afterwards it was because she had lost her own baby, which might have been true, but the woman was a stranger and there were rumours of a gang. However, nothing was proved and she got off with a fine, but Raoul has been fussy ever since. He just won't allow Michel to be taken from home unless he is well guarded.'

Eve gazed at her in bewilderment. 'But why should anyone wish to commit such a crime?'

'Money, usually,' Céleste shrugged. 'It happens all over the world. In France we are perhaps fortunate that such occurrences are rare. It is, as Raoul says, an international curse, projected by greed. Nevertheless, he won't take any chances.'

Which might excuse his rude behaviour in a way, although it still seemed ridiculous that he had suspected herself. 'If I went with you to the *manade*, and you introduced me yourself, then surely he would see sense?' Eve insisted.

'Not where you are concerned,' Céleste replied nervously. 'I have a great suspicion that he actually did realise who you are, because he has taken to lecturing me again about your family. So, for the moment, I dare not do anything!'

Eve tried to remain patient. 'But you must have had some plan when you contrived to get me here? You can't possibly have brought me all the way to France for nothing? After all, Raoul's dislike of my family is not altogether a new thing.'

'I had nothing definitely arranged,' Céleste confessed, lightly, much to Eve's disgust. 'I felt sure something would occur to me.'

Céleste's plans had always been like mirages in the desert, Eve recalled bitterly; she might have known!

'Actually, I have thought of something,' Céleste surprised Eve by continuing, if with some hesitation. 'There is a shallow lagoon, some miles away from the house, on the far side of the *mas*. We used to play there as children, Dominique and I. Sometimes Raoul came too, but then he was older. Our father built us a large hut for picnics and such and Raoul has always kept it in repair. It is a place where many rare birds are breeding, and occasionally I take Michel. The lagoon is not deep and he seems old enough to watch the birds and play a little by the water. To this Raoul does not object.'

'You mean,' Eve's face lit up eagerly, 'that I should meet you there, you and Michel?'

'I will do my best,' Céleste promised, 'but you must be careful. There are mudflats, ditches of brackish water which you won't be familiar with, and if any harm should befall you I should never get to Paris, I'm afraid.'

It might have been amusing, if her sense of humour had still been intact, to realise that Céleste's concern was entirely for her own plans. Yet Eve couldn't deny a small thrill of anticipation as she set out on her next afternoon off. After all, although this plan of Céleste's might prove crazy, anything was better than languishing at the hotel.

Céleste had given her clear instructions which she found fairly easy to follow. First the autobus to a certain point, then to follow a track to another point from which she should find it possible to see Céleste's car parked in the distance. The only thing to watch out for, Céleste had said, was perhaps a *gardian* rounding up cattle or horses, but it was unlikely that Eve would meet anyone that afternoon as most of the men were working on the other side of the ranch.

Bearing in mind Céleste's vagueness regarding the actual location of places, Eve wasn't greatly surprised to find the lagoon much further away from the road than she had been led to believe, and was both hot and irritated long before she reached it. But once there she did, to her relief, find Céleste, and the baby.

They were sitting outside the hut, Michel, now over a year old, playing happily while Céleste thumbed carelessly through the pages of a fashion magazine, taking little notice of the child by her side. For a moment Eve paused unseen, strangely moved as she watched soberly her irritation fast fading. He was a small, dark baby—a DuBare, not a bit like Carol until one noticed his eyes, which were large, and as warmly brown as hers had been. Eve felt her breath catch with a still aching sadness, a resentment against a fate which decreed that Céleste, who had no real interest in Michel, should be here instead of the mother who must have loved him dearly.

There came the noise of some laughter to her right, causing her to turn swiftly. Further along, shadowed by the tall grass which bordered the lagoon, were two men. They appeared to be elderly, their faces brown and wrinkled, creased in idle contemplation as they played cards, scarcely glancing at Eve as she stood apprehensively staring.

'It is all right, *chérie*, don't worry,' Céleste, having looked up and seen her, called gaily. 'It is only old François and Pierre from the *mas*. Raoul would never let me come here alone, but these men owe loyalty to me as well as him. They see nothing I don't wish them to.'

'Indeed!' Eve spoke sharply as she advanced, not at all happy about the situation in spite of Céleste's assurances. To have said these men gave her loyalty after her brother might have been nearer the mark, Eve suspected. However, there was nothing she could do but let it pass, and hope fervently that it might be at least partly true.

'Come and meet your nephew,' Céleste cried, her eyes indifferently amused on Eve's troubled face. 'I have no great feelings for so young a man, as you will know, but you will admit he is a darling, *n'est-ce pas?*'

But before Eve could reach them, or even had time to speak to the baby, to her horrified dismay there came the sound of a recklessly driven vehicle. Even Céleste's bright smile faded as the scream of heavily applied brakes pierced loudly through the overhanging trees, followed by the crash of a car door which must have rocked it on its hinges. 'Raoul!' Céleste started up, clutching Michel to her, blank surprise chasing the expression of supreme self-confidence from her small face. 'Oh, no!' she whispered, gazing helplessly at Eve. 'It can't be!'

But, unfortunately, it was. Striding through the scrub he came, around the corner of the hut, his face darker even than Eve remembered it. He looked positively dangerous, his mouth drawn thinly, and beneath his narrowed eyelids his light eyes glittered.

'*Mon dieu!*' he almost spat at his sister. 'So—when my back is turned this is how you repay my trust! Take yourself and the child back to the house at once. As for you, you scum,' he called with cold fury to the two old men, 'I will deal with you later, and do not hope I will forget.'

'And you, *mademoiselle*,' the ice in his eyes blazed to a burning anger when he allowed his glance to rest for one scorching moment on Eve's white face. 'You I will deal with immediately, as soon as I have seen my disreputable young sister on her way!'

'Oh, but, Raoul——!' At last Céleste seemed to find her tongue although she had obviously no clear idea as to how she might put things right. Her stumbling voice and frightened demeanour betrayed this. 'I don't think you should judge Eve too harshly. She only is interested in the baby.'

If Céleste had hoped to improve matters she had only succeeded in making the situation worse. The colour of controlled displeasure tautened Raoul DuBare's skin, leaving it marble-like in appearance, a coldness which caused Eve an inward shudder. 'Of that I have no doubt,' he agreed icily, 'but I beg of you, Céleste, go now, before I completely lose my temper. I do not wish to have to speak to you again!'

His temper! Eve's own anger, supplanting a little of her apprehension, raised scorn. Must he always be threatening people with the loss of a commodity he had too much of ever to run short of? Just in time she restrained herself from uttering her irrational thoughts aloud. The effort to hang on to her dignity was almost beyond her, yet she managed somehow to stand stiffly still while Céleste drove away with nothing more than an apologetic glance over her shoulder, the delicate implication that it was now up to Eve to make Raoul see sense. Clearly Céleste would be of little more help.

Her soft lips compressed, Eve turned warily to the man who stood, hands on hips over his skin-tight trousers, immensely tall in his leather boots. Her fair hair was swinging, blown by the wind across her eyes, hiding, she hoped, the sense of shock she experienced at the closeness of his presence. It was the same nerve-jerking sensation she had known before and, while she didn't understand it, it aroused vague fears which she found no easier to interpret. And because this surfeit of emotion seemed in some way to instigate a warning she tried, if unconsciously, to be sensible.

'Won't you please listen to me, Monsieur DuBare?' she said. 'I think,' she added, greatly daring, 'that you should. You can't possibly go on ignoring facts, or hope to change them by doing so.'

His eyes skimmed her face, not one whit relenting, and for one dreadful moment Eve felt he toyed with the notion of throwing her into the lagoon, and her own eyes flew with startled apprehension to the dark, reed-bound water.

'I should like to, *mademoiselle*, very much,' he assured her softly, with deadly accuracy reading her thoughts.

Eve swallowed painfully, trying to ignore the threat behind his words, choosing instead to repeat what she had just said, 'Won't you please listen?'

She was not prepared for the way in which his mouth thinned with contempt. 'So you would beg, *mademoiselle*— or bargain. Are you not able to make up your mind?'

Colour flamed, fanned by the taunting inflection in his smooth voice, to paint her pale cheeks vividly. 'I seldom resort to the first, *monsieur*, and never with you would I consider the second. It is not a case of being unable to make up my mind. I merely seek a logical solution.'

His hard lips continued to curl. 'And as you naturally suffer from the inherent stubbornness with which one automatically associates your race you won't take no for an answer. You are stubborn and pig-headed, and yet you expect me to be tolerant. Very well then, *mademoiselle*, I will consent to five minutes, no more. But it is I who will do the talking,' he finished enigmatically.

Without waiting for another comment he grasped her arm, the same arm which his forceful grip had bruised before, and where the marks of his fingers had long lingered. 'Come,' he said coldly, 'we will go into the hut. A little shade might help you deliver the speech you appear to have prepared in your head so diligently.'

'More quickly, you mean?' Eve gasped, knowing herself unheard as he thrust her almost rudely into the large wooden building only yards from where they stood.

If she had envisaged the inside of the hut at all she would have given it average proportions as there was nothing about the roughly hewn exterior to suggest the spaciousness and comfort she would find within. The floor was covered with cool green tiles and scattered rugs of a thick luxurious fur. There were small, glass-topped tables set near chair units deep with cushions, the material which covered them silken, obviously expensive. Soft glowing colours, reminding one of semi-precious stones, showed up intensely against the matt white paint of the walls, and across the windows hung curtains of the finest voile, shading delicately from creamy-white, yellow, pink and peach through to cyclamen.

It was beautiful, remarkable, a veritable oasis in a desert. Rather like an Eastern harem which someone had planned with care. And that someone could only have been Raoul DuBare. Not for the first time, in the short while she had known him, Eve felt her senses spin, and when she wrenched herself from his grasp and turned to face him she experienced all the terrors of a small, trapped animal.

CHAPTER THREE

For several minutes as Eve stared at Raoul DuBare the atmosphere seemed charged by an almost tangible distrust. Silence reigned, an uncomfortable silence, while Eve's thoughts raced alarmingly, her uneasiness quite clear to see. What did she really know of this man with his darkly compelling looks, his piratical manner? The trace of remoteness about him she found in no way reassuring. Rather it imbued a peculiar resentment that one so tall and solidly built should also contrive to possess such an air of elegance, denying as it did to his rough checked shirt and serviceable attire any claim to be the possessions of an ordinary worker.

Nothing stirred; the faint sound she heard could only have been the irregular thumping of her own heart. Outside there came only the occasional call of a bird, which seemed to emphasise their isolation, not detract from it. A shiver ran through Eve in spite of herself as his eyes went over her, lingering on her hair, as if considering its pale fairness, the damp, curling tendrils which had escaped the shining coil at her nape. Here was a man to notice, a man able, when he chose, to promote fear! Yet, as she met his assessing gaze, Eve was determined not to be browbeaten.

With impatient despair she tried to rally her wandering thoughts to decisive action. Such an opportunity as this might never again present itself, and here she was without apparently a word to say.

'I am waiting, *mademoiselle*,' he prompted, his eyes narrowed now on her hesitant face. 'If I allowed a mistaken sense of generosity to persuade me to hear you out, don't be tempted to try me too far. My patience is limited and I am a busy man.'

'But I don't have a great deal to say, *monsieur*,' she protested hurriedly. 'I only wish to insist that you don't continue to ignore the fact that I am Carol's cousin.'

'I wasn't aware she had one,' he stated impassively.

Eve started. Had Carol given this impression? It was difficult to believe and, even if for some unknown reason she had, there was surely the evidence of her husband and Céleste. 'Well, Carol's parents adopted me, but I really was her cousin, not her sister, and Carol always considered me one of the family. But then I've told you this before.'

'Indeed!' he gave the black-browed rejoinder more than a hint of incredulity. 'You'll have to do better than this, I'm afraid.'

He spoke in almost perfect English, with only the slightest intonation, otherwise Eve might have thought she hadn't heard aright. Was it possible that Carol had been forced to play down the actual size of her family in order to avoid Raoul DuBare's displeasure? '*Monsieur*,' she found herself exclaiming, 'I can't really fathom your determination to ignore plain facts, especially when you must know I can easily produce papers to prove my identity. Even if,' she added deliberately, remembering another day, 'I don't always carry such documents with me. Also, your sister knows me, and if you had spared her a moment she would have told you so. We were at school together—she stayed often at my uncle's house. It's not as if she had never seen me.'

His head came up, emphasising the taut line of his implacable jaw. 'So you keep saying, *mademoiselle*,' he taunted softly, 'and yet she fled like someone with a guilty conscience. I wonder why? I also wonder, *mademoiselle*, if you are who you say you are, what exactly you hope to achieve in coming here at this late hour.'

His question, coming as it did unexpectedly, reduced Eve to a state of some agitation, and, in faltering uncertainty, she made another mistake. Céleste hadn't yet given permission that her part in this affair should be disclosed. 'I wanted to see Michel,' she replied, deciding swiftly this was the line to take. 'My uncle, as you must know, is still an invalid in Rhodesia, and both he and my aunt worry about the boy as they are unable to visit. Not even you, *monsieur*, could insist that it is unnatural for them to be anxious about their only grandchild. So I, before going out to join them, agreed to at least try and see him.'

The glint in his eyes deepened dangerously as he studied her tense face, watching how the colour came and went beneath her flawless skin, giving her a curiously young, untouched look. Yet there was in his eyes, as they wandered to her delicately curved lips, a narrowed consciousness that here was no child but a woman, if an unawakened one.

'And if I refuse to let you see him?' he murmured almost absently, as if his mind explored other, more interesting possibilities.

For no reason at all, beneath his calculating glance, Eve's pulse jerked, causing her to assert more firmly than she intended, 'I must have some rights. Acting, as I should be doing, on behalf of Michel's grandparents, I'm quite sure I have, I'm also fairly sure there is nothing really much you can do about it, in spite of your fine talk!'

'You are impertinent, *mademoiselle*!' For one awful moment as his anger surged, Eve thought she had gone too far, but instantly he reverted to cool control, a sneering scorn. 'Whatever rights you or your family might imagine you have, I could sweep aside very quickly! Believe me, *mademoiselle*, I have gone into this matter very closely. Michel's place is here on the ranch where, when he is of age, he will inherit considerably—all that his father possessed, and more than probably, much of mine. No one you could name could offer so much or look after his interests so well. And let me warn you, *mademoiselle*, I am not a man to be threatened, not unless you are prepared to risk some form of retaliation.'

Whatever did he mean—retaliation? There was that in his face which suggested many things quite clearly. Eve felt her breath catch strangely in her throat and annoyed herself by taking a defensive step backwards. Not wholly aware of what she was saying, she cried, 'But you might have a family of your own! Even now you might have one?'

The phrasing of her sentence was so muddled as to be easily misconstrued. Again his eyes glinted. 'So you don't even know if I am married!' Triumph rang suavely. 'If you were familiar with my family then surely you would know this.'

'Of course I'm aware you aren't married!' Eve flushed, choking suddenly with the impatient, futile rage Raoul DuBare seemed able to arouse so easily, a rage, which after only two meetings, seemed to bring her to a state of hitherto unknown recklessness. 'And now that I've met you,' she cried, tears of despair almost blinding her eyes, 'I can well understand! I don't believe you have it in you to lead a normal married life! You're too full of ice! There's no understanding or tenderness in you anywhere. If you were to hold a girl in your arms you wouldn't know how to love her!'

Suddenly aghast, she trailed off to an almost indistinguishable whisper on her last three words. But he had heard all right—his face went hard and his eyes glittered, and she had never been so close to a man in such a cold fury before. In that crazy fraction of time, as he stood staring down at her, she would have given anything to have taken back what she had just said. On top of everything else to practically accuse him of being less than normal must seem the final insult. Whatever had made her utter such a lot of nonsense? She had no idea where such thoughts had come from—only a fool would ever think of Raoul DuBare as a celibate bachelor!

Something, not an intentional apology, escaped her cold lips unconsciously. 'I'm sorry,' she gasped, her cheeks stained red, her heart fluttering, 'I . . .'

Sharply he gave her no time to finish. Her voice faltered,

cut off in mid-sentence as his hands snaked out to grasp her shoulders, to pull her ruthlessly into his arms with a sureness and economy of movement that confirmed all her half formed doubts. There was a sensuousness, even in the touch of his hands, which Eve could not but be aware of as he held her to him.

His body was like steel, tough, and as he dragged her closer, the buttons and belt of his clothes pressed almost forcibly into her soft skin, hurting her. But her despairing wince went unnoticed as his hand went tightly to her slender neck, tilting her trembling mouth to meet his as his head came down.

Eve had never been kissed before, at least not like this. She supposed she had led a singularly chaste life, perhaps because she had been an unusually fastidious child, more interested in her immediate family and books. Mavis and George had never actively encouraged her to seek many friends of the opposite sex, being stricter with her than they had ever been with Carol, and Eve had always tried to please them by devoting herself firmly to her studies. In her dreams she had always imagined a man's arms would be wonderful, an experience she might cherish, but Raoul DuBare shattered such an illusion. His mouth on hers was unbelievably cruel, bruising her soft lips while she writhed and twisted in his arms in a desperate, unsuccessful attempt to free herself. Helpless, she was forced to endure his embrace until he chose to release her.

Yet for a moment, before he did so, she was still from sheer astonishment as something like quicksilver ran vividly through her. His arms held her tightly and with a kind of shameful confusion she became aware of the response of her body to every urgent nerve in his. It could only be that he sought to punish, but when he lifted his head she could scarcely find the strength to push him away.

Surprisingly his expression had changed slightly, a hint of speculation softening the derisive lines of his face as he

45

stared narrowly from her dazed eyes to her bruised, quivering mouth. 'You are still of the same opinion, *mademoiselle*?' he queried suavely.

'Opinion...?' Eve's voice came weakly. Through the peculiar tumult in her head she was not sure she had heard correctly. 'What opinion, *monsieur*?' she breathed, with the trembling air of one bemused.

'Do you deliberately misunderstand, or do you wish for even greater proof that I am a man?' he taunted dryly. His voice, unlike her own, was confidently smooth, and his words which should have shocked, raised instead a pleasurable, if wholly puzzling excitement. Deliberately enticing, he played on her young nerves with an experience he made no attempt to hide as again he lowered his dark head.

Eve couldn't turn away, even while conscious that in spite of a curious inclination to follow the dictates of her fast throbbing heart she must resist him. She was no child any more and, instinctively, she knew this man knew it. She merely lacked the experience which her traitorous body suddenly longed for, a knowledge of men which might have made her infinitely more exciting to someone like Raoul DuBare. As it was, she realised hazily, the situation could be fraught with danger. The lengthening shadows and fragrantly scented air of approaching evening played insidiously on the senses, doing nothing to assist her in her effort to pull herself from his arms.

His grasp on her cotton-clad shoulders tightened as he felt her resistance lessen. 'You make a very rewarding novice,' she heard him whisper, as his lips caressed the smooth fairness of her temples, exploring the soft curve of her cheek. 'I can be gentle, *ma petite*, should the need arise.'

'*Monsieur* ...!' Swiftly, as the taunting softness of his voice smote her, she tore herself resolutely away, convulsively ashamed of her over responsive body. Raoul was almost a complete stranger; that she had gone to school with his sister could be no excuse. Lost for further words, she

46

stared at him, her blue-green eyes wide. Any claim to dignity she had possessed must be lost for ever, yet surely no humiliating scene need be prolonged to the extent of becoming painful. Somehow she seemed to have lately acquired the unhappy knack of getting herself into awkward situations, but no one, she felt sure, could have foreseen this. '*Monsieur*,' she tried again, 'you must excuse me. I will return to my hotel.'

His white teeth glinted as if he took pleasurable satisfaction from her strained, slightly haunted expression as she stared into his face. 'And you, *mademoiselle*,' he remarked, with a coolness she envied, 'must discontinue telling me what I may or may not do. That I have found a way of silencing your eloquence very considerably is something I intend to keep in mind.'

'I'm sorry—there were things I had no right to say.' For an instant Eve's thick lashes flickered as she felt the apology tremble involuntarily from her lips. Did he have to stand there looking so wholly superior, his eyes, like a light flame, licking over her, missing nothing, carelessly cynical.

His head inclined the merest fraction, autocratically, as if he accepted her humbled gesture as his due. 'I will take you back to your hotel, *mademoiselle*, if you would be so kind as to tell me where you are staying? I'm afraid I have no idea.'

And he had never tried to find out. After their first, stormy encounter at the ranch he must have considered himself well and truly rid of her, otherwise, she guessed with sudden conviction, he would have made it his business to discover her whereabouts. Somehow, unpredictably, the knowledge hurt. 'There is no need to take me anywhere, Monsieur DuBare,' she stressed his name deliberately. 'I found my way here. I can just as easily find my way back.'

'You would enjoy thinking even less of me should I let you?' he taunted.

Again her colour flared in creamy cheeks. '*Monsieur*, I've said I'm sorry.'

'Not very convincingly.'

'And you're a man who must have his pound of flesh twice over!' she cried impetuously.

One black eyebrow rose sardonically. 'Don't quote your bards to me, *mademoiselle*, I am not in the mood!'

Eve noticed he still refrained from calling her anything else but *mademoiselle*, which seemed to emphasise his suspicions, each time he uttered it, of her true identity. Nervously filled with an odd trembling resentment, she turned from him, making for the door. 'I will accept your offer, *monsieur*,' she acquiesced, without meaning to, subconsciously desperate to escape. 'I forgot to ask the time of the returning bus. I intended to ask Céleste.'

He followed her from the hut before answering, turning the key in the lock before thrusting it deep into his pocket as if something about the building irritated him. His shrug as he turned to her again seemed suddenly very Gallic, warning her forcibly that he was alien, not one of her own countrymen, but she felt too strung up to let it bother her. Maybe he was recalling other more amorously rewarding episodes in the hut beside which her own reluctant responses compared unfavourably?

'Céleste,' he was grunting, 'would merely have told you that there was no guarantee that the bus would return, and then left you to find out for yourself. It would be well, *mademoiselle*, that you do not expect too much of my sister.'

Was that a threat—or a warning? There was no telling. Glancing despairingly at his hard profile as he expertly drove his heavy vehicle through the dense scrub, Eve was intensely aware of how little she really knew of this man who had just kissed her so roughly. She disliked him, and everything and everyone to do with him! Impulsively her mind made numerous decisions. None of them—neither Céleste, or George and Mavis—could expect more of her! She couldn't bear to stay here any longer; she would tell Mrs Wood.

The vehicle sped—driven violently. She had a good excuse,

if one was needed, as they bumped madly over the uneven ground, not to make any comment on his sarcastic statement. There was, anyway, no point in discussing anything with Raoul DuBare any more. His mind had been made up long before she had ever arrived. Her feeble persistence hadn't changed one thing, only annoyed him and strengthened his resolve to keep Michel away from his mother's family.

Mulling over this sullenly, Eve was surprised to hear him say just before they reached the hotel, 'Carol's father ... Has he recovered at all from his heart attack?'

'Not really, *monsieur*,' she replied stiffly, unable, because her head felt so numb, to reconcile his remark with his persistent refusal to acknowledge that she was Carol's cousin.

Yet he went further, if rather obviously against his will. 'They have not yet returned home?'

Still stiffly, Eve murmured, keeping her eyes determinedly on the road, 'The doctors don't advise it—besides, they can't afford to risk it, not at the moment.'

'I do not follow.'

Eve sighed, her brow troubled in spite of her resolve to present an indifferent front. She said reluctantly, 'They like it out there, and, if England had an adverse effect on George's health, they couldn't afford to return.'

'I see ...'

Something calculated in his words caused her to glance at him with sudden suspicion. It was as if he deliberately probed for information that pleased him. Yet how could this be? Then almost as if he read her thoughts and wished to banish them from her mind, he attacked deviously, as she indicated vaguely towards the hotel.

'You may complain about a lack of money, *mademoiselle*, but you appear to be doing yourself very well!'

'How do you mean?' Again she floundered uncertainly, bewildered by his changing tones.

'Living here,' he waved a sarcastic hand towards Mrs Wood's large, modern establishment, 'how many weeks?'

'Almost four.'

'Mrs Wood's hotel is not the cheapest, being almost first class.'

The implication was suddenly quite clear. Eve's skin prickled with angry resentment as he drove swiftly into the car park and, before he had quite stopped, she wrenched open the door and jumped stumbling on to the tarmac. It made no difference that he watched her untimely flight with dark eyebrows raised, nor that Mrs Wood, on one of her never-ending promenades, was coming around the corner, her eyebrows elevated almost as high as Raoul DuBare's.

'Thank you, *monsieur*,' Eve gasped as her breath choked. 'What you point out is no doubt true, but you may be sure I won't trouble you again—and that when I go I will leave no debts that might sully, even indirectly, your illustrious name!'

'*Au revoir, mademoiselle*,' he returned grimly, as with an indifferent lift of his hand to Mrs Wood he drove away.

'And what were you doing driving with Monsieur DuBare?' Mrs Wood pounced almost before he was out of sight.

In vain Eve tried to hide her hot cheeks. She could see quite clearly that Mrs Wood felt rather slighted because Raoul DuBare had not stopped to speak and, now that he had gone, Eve had no wish to discuss him. Nor did she want Mrs Wood to know she knew him or any of his family. 'He merely gave me a lift,' she forced herself to prevaricate. 'I missed the bus.'

If she had hoped to divert Mrs Wood easily she was doomed to disappointment. Mrs Wood's eyes and wits, sharpened by many years in business, saw through her small subterfuge. 'Raoul DuBare,' she persisted suspiciously, 'does not make a habit of picking people up, especially strange girls. I do hope, my dear, you haven't been indiscreet? I must think of the reputation of my hotel.'

To Eve's chagrin she felt her flush deepen, until she felt an expression of guilt must be written all over her. It was little use trying to convince herself that Mrs Wood's unfortunate phrasing was entirely responsible for the warmth in her cheeks. What, she wondered unhappily, would Mrs Wood have thought could she have known what had happened in the hut by the lagoon? But there were some things Eve had no wish to recall, not even to herself. 'I can assure you, Mrs Wood,' she managed, 'that Monsieur DuBare is in no way interested in me!'

Partly mollified by the vehement emphasis in Eve's tones, Mrs Wood's doubts appeared to leave her, and when she continued it was with a surprising archness. 'You see, dear, he is a man with a considerable reputation regarding the fair sex, and I do feel in some way responsible for you. You couldn't have known this, of course, when you accepted his offer of a lift.'

'I wouldn't know, naturally,' Eve replied shortly as, in an attempt to escape, she turned to walk away. In spite of herself a flicker of dry humour smote her. Mrs Wood seemed to imply that Raoul DuBare was a kind of highwayman, lying in wait for unsuspecting victims by the roadside. She wondered curiously what he would have made of such an exaggerated impression, and shuddered to imagine the sarcasm of his indifferent comments. 'I don't think I shall see Monsieur DuBare again,' she added, deliberately.

Mrs Wood walked with her, obviously, even while satisfied her fears had proved groundless, not willing to be diverted. 'He's reputed to be well off, certainly he's a man of some property, but apart from this, his looks and personality make him much sought after.'

'But I'm not in the least interested in Monsieur DuBare, Mrs Wood!' Of a sudden the drama of the afternoon combined with Mrs Wood's tenacious attack caused Eve's voice to tremble. 'I hadn't the faintest notion that he's wealthy.'

'Just because he rides with his own *gardians* and often wears the same rough clothing, people are apt to be misled. They say he can work harder than his men when he takes it into his head, but this shouldn't hide the fact that he's equally experienced when it comes to women.'

Uneasily Eve stared at her employer with barely concealed astonishment. It didn't seem possible that Mrs Wood was more than a little interested in Raoul DuBare herself, and Eve couldn't help wondering what it was about him that attracted women so helplessly. 'Why hasn't he married,' she asked scornfully, 'as he's so popular?'

Mrs Wood shrugged. 'He's apparently not in any hurry. There is an heir, of course, his late brother's son, so he possibly feels there's no urgency in that direction. A Frenchman, more than many others, sets great store by a son and heir, so eventually I expect he will get around to marrying and having a family of his own. There has been a rumour about a girl who occasionally comes and stays.'

'I see . . .' Eve said thoughtfully.

'You must excuse me, dear.' Mrs Wood's secretary was waving, and business must always come first, even before the fascinating DuBares. Mrs Wood ran, leaving Eve gazing unhappily after her.

Later that same evening there was a telephone message. It was Céleste, although she didn't give her name until Eve picked up the receiver. For one awful moment Eve had thought it might be bad news from Rhodesia, but instead of relief she knew only anger that she should be made to suffer even momentarily through the DuBares again. 'What is it?' she asked coldly, her voice clearly unfriendly as she resisted the impulse not to speak to Céleste at all.

'I had to ring, Eve.' She apologised briefly for her part in the fiasco of the afternoon, before having the audacity to add, 'When you come to know Raoul better you will realise he is not too bad.'

'I don't want to listen while you sing your brother's praises,' Eve retorted, feeling she'd had more than enough from Mrs Wood.

'Please,' Céleste cried shrilly, apparently alarmed, 'don't ring off. Raoul has had to leave for Paris—an emergency has blown up. I must not see you until he returns, he says, but when he comes home he will arrange to bring you here, to the ranch. He is prepared, he told me, to discuss certain things, although he would not divulge exactly what.'

'I'm afraid,' Eve said stonily, 'I won't be here.'

'Oh, please, *chérie*,' Céleste begged, 'do not go away, you must not! I don't know what you said to Raoul, but you seem to have made quite an impression. He has been strange all evening, as if he has much on his mind. This might be just the opportunity we are looking for to arrange something for Michel.'

'I'll think about it,' Eve answered tonelessly, and, without giving the girl a chance to say anything more, she quickly replaced the receiver. Her few words had been deliberately misleading. She had no intention of going within miles of the ranch ever again. Wild horses, not even Camargue ones, she reflected with a mirthless grin, could drag her within miles of the place! She intended to leave at the end of the week. If she had still been a guest she would have left in the morning, but, as things stood, she did owe Mrs Wood some sort of notice.

But unfortunately Mrs Wood considered Eve owed her much more notice than a few days. When Eve tentatively announced that she must return to London almost immediately she met with icy displeasure. Mrs Wood was furious and made little attempt to hide her anger. 'I simply can't allow you to walk out on me like this,' she exclaimed. 'And it's not as if you have another job to go to. You must stay until the end of the month,' she commanded, dismissing Eve from her office with a decisive wave of her hand.

Perhaps she was right, Eve reflected gloomily. As an employer, Mrs Wood must have certain rights, and she did have her hotel to think about. In her position she wouldn't be given to quoting untrue facts which might easily be refuted. 'Very well,' she shrugged, giving in unhappily, but realising there was no other thing she could do.

During the next week Eve worked extremely hard, and if

53

she had her suspicions that Mrs Wood deliberately found her more to do than was necessary she proudly made no protest. Mrs Wood might shout and bully, but Eve determined to keep her dignity intact. Yet there were days when she felt almost weighed down beneath the sheer numbers of children she was expected to supervise, and when the rest of the staff whispered that she was being 'put upon' she found it difficult not to succumb to their obvious sympathy. To keep a stiff upper lip had never seemed harder, but what other alternative did she have? And, as Mrs Wood had so ruthlessly pointed out, she had nothing really to return to. In spite of all the hard work she was probably wiser to stay. Her salary, though not generous, was good. If she saved most of it by doing without the extra meals she had got into the habit of buying outside, the small nest-egg she would consequently acquire would come in very useful when she did eventually return to England.

It was then, just as she began to imagine hopefully he had forgotten about her, that she heard from Raoul DuBare. It was in the form of a brief note from Paris. In it he said he was returning to the ranch and would see her next day. It was signed with equal abruptness—DuBare, and Eve stared at it in some dismay, wondering apprehensively why even the sight of his dark, masculine handwriting had the power to accelerate her heartbeats. It was almost as if he had appeared in person, actually confronting her. Why had he chosen to write? Of course, while he could have more easily contacted her by telephone initially she would not have answered herself and other people would have known. This, she was convinced, he would not want. Yet a note was merely a note, there was nothing to stop her from pretending she had not received it. It would do him no harm to discover not everyone was ready and willing to obey him, and he must know as well as she that there was absolutely nothing left for them to talk about.

Much later in the day she was still reassuring herself that she didn't have to go, scarcely aware that the note she had stuffed in her pocket was almost worn to fragments by constant re-reading. It didn't seem possible, in the face of such resolute determination, that she should find herself on the following afternoon clinging to the seat of a recklessly speeding bus on her way to the ranch.

Fortunately it was her regular evening off. Mrs Wood had asked her to work, but for once Eve had been adamant, even daring to say she was going an hour earlier than usual—a statement which had met with such a frigid reception that in the frozen silence she had managed to escape before Mrs Wood had had time to question such a frivolous disregard of duty. Eve knew instinctively that she would never have got away had Mrs Wood had the vaguest idea where she was going to.

It wasn't until some time after the bus set her down that Eve discovered she was much further from the ranch than she had thought. Distance, in such a wilderness, she realised, must be deceptive. On her first visit she had hired one of Mrs Wood's cars and had seemed to reach the ranch quickly. When she had met Céleste at the lagoon it had been almost completely in the other direction. Now she found the vast plains curiously frightening, the size of them dwarfing her like a small dot in a seemingly limitless region of scrub and water. She had travelled a good way from the hotel, some twenty miles, she guessed, but otherwise she had little idea exactly where she was. To her right she saw water buttercups spreading like white carpets across sheets of water, and on her other side, windswept steppes, covered with salt grass. She shivered, concentrating on the dry land rather than the marshes where she remembered Céleste once mentioned wild boar lurked. Noticing the reeds, the thick clumps of bulrushes, she could quite believe it.

The sun was hot, too hot for comfort, and with it the inevitable mistral was blowing which bothered Eve even more than the heat. Fortunately the rough road was well marked so she couldn't get lost, but with each step she became more and more convinced she had been crazy to even think of coming here. Even to think of Raoul DuBare filled her with a painful confusion, a growing certainty, where he was concerned, of her own vulnerability.

One heel was badly blistered and her thin cotton dress clung damply to her skin long before she reached the ranch-house and wearily climbed the now familiar steps, the extra effort required to do so making her feel quite peculiar. Possibly Raoul wouldn't be in and she would be forced to wait in the warm kitchen until he condescended to appear. Already she fancied she knew him well enough to be able to foretell clearly how he would treat her.

Eve knocked, and, contrary to her expectations, the door opened almost immediately, and a dark, pleasant-looking young woman appeared. Eve spoke in French, imagining it would be quicker, and was rewarded by a swift smile.

'Ah, yes, *mademoiselle*,' the woman nodded, as Eve asked for Monsieur DuBare, 'he thought you might come here. I am to take you to him at once. My name is Marie,' she concluded sedately.

'But why shouldn't I come here, is this not where he lives?' Eve asked with surprise, as Marie stepped outside, closing the door quickly behind her. Marie merely shook her shining black head, beckoning that Eve should follow.

It was difficult to argue with the temperature so high and feeling as she did. It was all she could do to walk back down the uneven stone steps without tumbling to the bottom in an undignified heap. Not for the first time that afternoon Eve deplored the fact that she hadn't come by car. Quite easily, if she hadn't become obsessed by the need to save money, she could have hired one, and could now have returned to the hotel until she felt better, or at least to some not so distant spot until she had managed to pull herself together.

At the bottom of the steps Marie paused, glancing doubt-fully back over her shoulder at Eve's pale face, then, as if deciding that all Englishwomen must look like wilting violets, she continued on around the corner of the building, making for a thick clump of trees a short way off. There was poplar, Eve noticed, and ash, some elm and alder, all fully in leaf. She was astonished to find such luxuriant growth here in an area which seemed mostly covered by low scrub. Through the trees, as they drew nearer, she glimpsed a house, a long, low structure painted in a beautiful clean white, set in the midst of gardens gay with flowers, again in direct contrast to the arid countryside around them.

Eve found herself blinking as she entered the imposing front door. Mrs Wood had not been exaggerating; Raoul DuBare must indeed be a man of some substance to run a place like this! In direct contrast to the warmth outside the interior was tiled and cool and, as Marie directed her into a drawing room she noticed the eighteenth-century French furniture, the Chinese porcelain, Samarkand rugs. She longed suddenly to sink into one of the deep sofas, draped with furs. The sensuous luxury beckoned almost irresistibly, and it was only by concentrated effort that she remained on her own two feet. Marie said, 'I will go now and seek Monsieur Raoul,' but Eve scarcely heard her leaving, and was startled, a few minutes later, to find him standing by her side.

'So—you have arrived,' he said smoothly, his keen glance flicking her closely, his voice dry—as if he never, for one moment, had doubted she would come.

For an instance Eve made no response. She was too sensitive. Already she had realised the futility of resenting this man's ability to bruise and deflate. Glancing at him swiftly, her eyes darkening, she strove to keep her face in the shadows, that he might not read the quiver that ran across it.

'You have the evidence of your own eyes, *monsieur*,' she tried to lace her own tongue with some of his light sarcasm, 'but I believe I was extremely foolish to come ...'

Abruptly he cut in, 'That, Mademoiselle Reston, will remain to be seen. I in turn could be regretting that I sent for

57

you, but once you are gone I must be satisfied I am rid of you completely. I do not intend, at some future date, that my conscience should suggest I made a mistake.'

Eve felt nothing but scorn for his enigmatical statement. 'It is good to know you have a conscience, *monsieur*, whichever way it works, but not that you consider it the only reason for dragging me all the way here!' When she considered all those endless miles in the sun she could cheerfully have hit him. But her soft vehemence spoke for itself, as did the tenseness of her slight body, the smouldering heat in her wide blue eyes.

He shrugged, apparently discounting anything she might have suffered. 'I regret, *mademoiselle*,' he bowed slightly, dryly, 'if I have caused you any inconvenience, but I have only just arrived from Paris myself, having been unavoidably held up. As a matter of fact I was about to ring your hotel to tell you that I would send a car when Marie told me you were already here. I know, of course, that you have your own car, and while I agree it is quite a distance, you had surely nothing else to do.'

Eve ignored this with difficulty, not willing to give him the satisfaction of knowing how far she had walked. He had called her by her actual name, even though he had quickly reverted to the more anonymous *mademoiselle*, which must be a sign that he half believed her story.

If only her head would clear, then this last interview might be made to justify all the humiliation she was suffering in coming here today. Everything about this man seemed, for no sensible reason, to be becoming too personal! This was merely their third meeting, yet he appeared to have the power to hurt her in a deeply disturbing way.

Eve's fraught emotions whirled, and, in flare of unconscious despair, she wished fervently to escape from him. Michel's fate must be dealt with promptly. 'Please,' she begged, agitation quickening her tones, 'what exactly did you want to see me about?'

CHAPTER FOUR

Eve's query, put so nervously, hung between them tentatively for several seconds before Raoul answered. 'You must know, *mademoiselle*, that I wished to see you about Michel. There could be nothing else.'

Eve flushed, in spite of an all-prevailing numbness. There was in his voice a slight insolence which she found difficult to assimilate. He surely didn't imagine she had hoped there could be anything else? That she had expected an apology for his uncouth behaviour when they had last met beside the lagoon? Men like Raoul DuBare, she sensed instinctively, never apologised for kissing a girl, not even as he had done. 'I am quite aware, *monsieur*, there could only be Michel, but just a short while ago you refused to discuss anything about him. I'm simply curious to know why you should change your mind.'

'Let me put it this way,' he drawled suavely, 'you have already condemned me as a brute, and long before a certain—er—incident occurred, but I put it to you that your own manner of approach has been far from straightforward. If you are who you say you are—and I have more reason now to believe you are speaking the truth—then I think you owe me some sort of explanation—as to why you arrived on that first day as you did, the veil of secrecy you chose to draw over your initial approach.'

With an air of slight desperation, Eve hedged, still reluctant to implicate Céleste. 'Would anything have made any difference?' she remonstrated. 'You've always refused to see me.'

'You probably don't realise,' he said curtly, 'that once an attempted kidnapping was conducted in almost exactly the same manner. A woman, not an English one, forced her way in here when Michel was but a few weeks old. It was only because of Marie's vigilance that she did not succeed.'

'But surely——' Eve whispered, as shock ran through her.

'Perhaps,' he continued, interrupting without apology, 'you can imagine how I felt when you appeared!'

'But I did tell you,' Eve protested, unwilling to accept what she was convinced was only half of the truth, 'and you had only to ask Céleste.'

'Yes,' he nodded grimly. 'In fact I have consulted my sister, but she has been almost as devious as you.'

Quite helplessly, Eve sat down. He hadn't asked her to, and, conscious of what seemed a deliberate omission, she had been determined in spite of a feeling of faintness to stand, but of a sudden her legs just refused to support her. 'Please,' she whispered, her eyes dilating strangely with terror, 'I must return to the hotel. I feel terrible—my head . . .'

For fully a minute he took no notice, remaining where he was, a few feet distant, his dark gaze narrowed cynically on her lightly perspiring face. 'I suppose,' he taunted dryly, 'this is all part of the act. Now that you feel you have established your identity, you announce that you are ill, possibly hoping to gain an invitation to stay until you are quite recovered.'

'Why, you fiend . . .!' Through a hazy whirl of colour which danced confusingly before her eyes. Eve was unable to see the calculating sneer on his face, but she knew it would be there. How could he ever imagine she would wish to stay when she would have given anything to have been able to get to her feet and walk out—and never come back! She couldn't even find the strength to continue her involuntary attack, her few furious words petering out as another wave of sickness hit her. 'Please, *monsieur*,' she pleaded, aghast, 'you'd better get someone to drive me back to the hotel, otherwise I won't be responsible. It must have been the sun.'

'The sun?' he rasped. 'How could that be?'

But Eve was past answering. Unable to stop herself, she

sank back, letting herself be enveloped in the depth of the sofa, her head slipping to one side, drunkenly, her face paper-white against the soft green velvet.

'*Mon dieu!*' he ground out, beside her in one stride, his fingers swiftly on her wrist, his head blocking out the light. His fingertips on her pulse seemed almost professional. '*Mon dieu!*' he repeated, 'what have you been doing with yourself?'

'I walked too far, I think,' Eve forced herself to reply through shaking lips as the room whirled in a most peculiar fashion about her. She bit her lip hard, knowing that all of a sudden her eyes were full of over emotional tears. 'Please,' she begged, with a slight movement of her head, 'won't you just take me home?' Home, at that moment, was not the hotel, nor even London, it was the small town where she had grown up. She had a sudden longing for it.

He naturally thought she meant the hotel. 'No, not there,' he exclaimed, unexpectedly curt. 'Obviously, although Mrs Wood's establishment is good, the air there must not suit you.' His eyes swept her slight figure. 'You look as though a slight breeze would blow you down. When did you last have anything to eat?'

'This morning,' she muttered, scarcely daring to speak for fear the nausea overtook her. 'I shall be quite all right, *monsieur*, if you would only do as I ask.'

'And who is going to look after you?'

Eve ignored the savage emphasis in his voice, just as she hoped she hadn't heard aright when he shouted loudly for Marie. Her eyes, enormous, like rainwashed blue skies, fastened on him despairingly, and she couldn't control the trembling unhappiness which shook her limbs. Why wouldn't he listen? The expression on his face was so cynical she could have cried. Why didn't he just throw her out when he wasn't duty bound, or inclined, to do anything else?

Then suddenly there was a glass in his hand and she

found herself hauled up against his hard male frame, and he forced her to drink while Marie hovered. His hand came firmly behind her head and the brandy stung her lips, making her choke. Wildly she tried to turn away, the fineness of her hair spilling over his wrist like silk, shaken, even while feeling so ill, by a primitive determination to resist him.

She might well have been a small child wrestling with someone of infinitely more experience. He controlled her feeble struggles by merely tightening his grip on her slender shoulders while he swiftly instructed Marie, 'Mademoiselle Eve appears to be suffering from exhaustion as well as the sun. We will put her to bed and see how she feels in the morning. The Blue Room, I think. The colours there are cool and she might feel a certain affinity which might help her head.'

How did he manage to insert so much hidden mockery into a simple statement? Marie, with an anxious if slightly bewildered smile, was gone in an instant, presumably to turn down the bed, and Eve knew a moment of blind, unreasonable panic. Illness was no excuse; she must not be persuaded to stay in this place, with this man. 'No, no!' she cried, attempting unsuccessfully to sit up so he might see she was not in need of such attention. 'You can't be sure,' she added weakly, 'I'm suffering from exhaustion.'

As she had half expected, he took not the least bit of notice. 'Isolated as we are in the Camargue,' he grunted, 'a *manadier* must be knowledgeable about such things—a layman's knowledge, if you like, *mademoiselle*, but one that not many of us could manage without. Besides, *le docteur* is a busy man, we do not call him unless necessary. My men often consult me first before the doctor. This is why I venture to conclude that you are merely suffering from some kind of exhaustion and require chiefly rest. As I have said, we will possibly be able to judge better in the morning.'

When I might well be dead, Eve thought, curiously contradictory. She winced, touching a hand to her temple. It was pounding abominably, burning hot too. She felt vaguely sorry for herself and oddly resentful that he should sound so coolly unsympathetic, even while he offered a bed.

'Stop fighting,' he ordered, suddenly decisive, as if her odd murmurings of protest irritated him beyond endurance. 'I have had a busy day and, as yet, can see no end to it. Come.'

Was it her imagination or was there actually a thread of tenderness in his voice on that last word, or was it simply in his arms as he lifted her, a normal but impersonal compassion as he carried her from the room? Even to be lifted brought back the terrible dizziness and she found herself clinging to him in an aching, suffocating silence, wholly grateful for the cool smoothness of his elegant town suit against the heat of her cheek.

'Marie,' she heard him speaking, but in such rapid French it was impossible to follow. She was dimly aware that the woman came with them upstairs and was assuring Raoul earnestly that she had found a suitable negligé for Mademoiselle and would most gladly help her into bed.

'And do not argue, Eve,' he said lightly, as he strode into a bedroom and laid her carefully on soft cool sheets. 'You're in no condition, and you'll soon feel more comfortable if you leave everything to Marie.'

When he took his arms away Eve felt strangely lost and unconsciously clasped hot fingers on his sleeve as if to detain him. 'I'll be back,' he fixed his dark gaze on her, his face enigmatically grim as he noticed how the whiteness of the pillow almost matched the colour of her face. 'In a few moments,' he promised, releasing her slim hand.

He was. She was scarcely between the sheets before he returned, in his hand a glass of water and some tablets. 'Two of these will enable you to get a good night's rest,' he said, and Eve was helplessly ashamed to find herself submitting meekly to his firm administrations. She swallowed the tablets as if anxious for the oblivion they might bring, so that she might no longer see how his coolly assessing glance swept over her.

It was an effort to speak through the throbbing pain in her head, but she did manage to say hoarsely, 'In an hour I shall probably have recovered, at least enough to go back to the hotel. Mrs Wood will be wondering where I've got to. Perhaps Marie would be kind enough to wake me up?'

'You won't be going anywhere this evening,' Raoul Du-Bare retorted, Eve's persistence obviously irritating. 'As for the good Mrs Wood, I shall see to it personally that she is informed of your whereabouts. Naturally she will be worried to lose one of her guests, but it is a simple matter of picking up the telephone. I will see to it at once, so you might relax, *mademoiselle*.'

Eve's eyes, too large for her face, stared up at him in dismay. He must not be allowed to contact Mrs Wood—she must find the right words to stop him. But already the sleeping pills were at work, her lashes drooped, too heavy to lift again, even slightly. There was a somewhat muddled plan in her mind as to what she must do. She must ask Marie to find Céleste—she must ask Céleste to deter her brother from ringing Mrs Wood. She must . . . but whatever else it was Eve never knew as, with a wholly indifferent disregard of her efforts to stay awake, sleep overtook her.

It was morning before she woke, and to her surprise found Céleste perched on the end of her bed, appraising her pensively.

'Oh, good!' the girl exclaimed, when Eve opened her eyes. 'I thought you weren't going to, ever. Do you know what time it is? It is after midday, *chérie*. You have almost slept the clock around.'

Momentarily Eve couldn't remember a thing. She hadn't the faintest idea where she was or what Céleste was talking about? Then, because she hadn't been actually hurt in any way, it all came rushing back. The humiliating way she had almost collapsed into Raoul's arms and how he had ignored her struggles and carried her here and doped her ruthlessly with sleeping tablets when she had dared to protest! At least, in the light of her rising annoyance, this construction seemed reasonably correct. Gingerly she felt her head with nervous, exploratory fingers. The ache was still there, but only dully, the nausea was gone. Yet she still felt strangely tired in spite of sleeping—what had Céleste just said, almost the clock around?

Surely not? Aghast, she tried to sit up, while Céleste watched her feeble contortions with a kind of detached interest. 'Raoul is right,' she observed aloud and with faint astonishment, 'you are quite attractive when you are not all starched up. That nightgown, *chérie*, never can I recall you wearing anything like it. Even your cotton dresses always managed to appear—how is it you say, old-fashioned.'

As she digested what she presumed were Raoul DuBare's remarks, Eve felt her cheeks flush scarlet, and exhausted by a surge of dismay she collapsed again against her pillows. Rather incredulously she glanced down at the brief wisp of satiny material which Céleste referred to as a nightgown. Had Raoul DuBare really seen her like this? As he had put her to bed, he must have done, but it didn't bear thinking about! She swallowed a nervous lump in her throat, beset by an odd trembling.

'This nightgown, Céleste, as you must know, is probably yours, and I have never been able to afford very much in the way of clothes. You must be aware that a student is usually hard up, and besides, it has never mattered much how I dressed. I've always tried to be tidy.'

'Which at your age should not be something to boast about, Mademoiselle Reston.'

Through Céleste's small squeal of laughter, Eve's eyes swung to collide with Raoul DuBare's as he stood in the doorway and her breath caught raggedly in her throat at his sheer vitality. He was dressed this morning in a pair of

65

casual but well tailored cream trousers which he wore with a cool silk shirt, a cravat knotted with careless elegance circling his brown neck. She was struck anew by his absolute physical presence, the almost tangible strength of the man, because there was something physical about him, a prevailing masculinity she had never encountered in one of her own countrymen. Helplessly she shuddered. Her instincts had warned her, had they not, on their first encounter to be wary, but what possible defence did a girl have against such a dynamic personality? Yet she did try, when at last she found her voice, to assert herself a little.

'I don't think you have the right to criticise my appearance, Monsieur DuBare,' she exclaimed.

'Not under normal circumstances,' he agreed mildly as he moved into the room, 'but you must admit that since you arrived circumstances have been far from that.'

'Which does give him a certain licence,' Céleste added gaily, before Eve could speak.

'That will be enough from you, *chérie*,' Raoul warned his sister, although his voice retained its prevalent mildness.

He turned again to the girl in the bed, studying her narrowly, his gaze wandering without haste from the ruffled strands of her pale hair to where the slender straps of her diaphanous attire clung transparently to her slender shoulders. There was an odd flicker in the back of his dark eyes, something Eve had noticed before—dislike, perhaps, but it was enough to cause her heart to begin hammering relentlessly at her ribs, and make the blood go racing through her body. It brought a hectic flush to cheeks still too lacking in colour, a wild resentment that this man could have such an effect on her, and defensively aware of his intent regard, she gathered the white coolness of the sheet tightly around her.

Raoul saw the flush which painted her smooth skin and misconstrued it. 'I didn't wish to disturb you until you felt better, Eve. There are things I would rather leave until another day, but I can see that until we have certain matters cleared up you will not rest as you should.'

He glanced swiftly to Céleste. 'You may make yourself scarce until Eve and I have talked, but first you can bring her a shawl, something she might wear until such a time she does not feel it necessary to cover herself up.'

Eve had never felt so confused before. His audacity was almost unbelievable! She tried to raise her eyes to look at him steadily, only to find his green ones looking down at her, a glitter in their depths that made her quake inwardly. Even the smile which just touched his hard mouth was not the least humorous. There was something calculating about it, oddly menacing which in no way steadied her racing pulses.

Inside her moved a desire to spring out of bed, if only her legs had not appeared to be held down by leaden weights and her head still too fuzzy to direct a clear course of action. Céleste had rushed to do his bidding in a whirl of sweetly innocent alacrity. Between the two of them she might have little chance of surviving if she didn't watch out!

The bedjacket arranged, Céleste retreated with what she seemed to imagine was an encouraging smile, but one which Eve couldn't for the life of her return. The girl, like her brother, appeared, singularly lacking in conscience. Hadn't it been Céleste who had got her into all this trouble and who, from the look of things, was not willing to lend even one hand to help her out!

Wordlessly Eve stared mutinously at her own hands while Raoul drew forward a chair and placed it beside her. 'Do you feel better now, Eve?' he inquired, disregarding her silence, the slight sulkiness which emphasised the wide curves of her mouth.

'I'm not sure,' she responded reluctantly, not sure if he referred to the bedjacket or her health. She decided on the latter. 'I think I should feel better once I was up,' she suggested pointedly.

He merely shook his head. 'In a few minutes Marie will bring you a light lunch and straighten your bed, then you must rest again until this evening. Only then, if you feel well enough, may you get up, perhaps for dinner.'

'You can't keep me a prisoner here!'

'No?' his smile was slight and this time faintly mocking as he glanced around the charming room. 'There are those women, my dear, who have enjoyed being kept prisoner in a bedroom, but I will promise that you may come down for your evening meal if you in turn will promise to do as you are told until then.'

Why did he have always to taunt her inexperience? Obviously the women he knew had a sophistication to match his own and wouldn't be troubled by inhibitions such as hers. Desperately she tried to keep her mind on other things. 'I am not an invalid,' she insisted stiffly, 'nor can I guess why you should choose to turn me into one, *monsieur.*'

'Raoul...' he corrected, gently but firmly, his eyes glinting as her slight body visibly flinched, her curved breasts tautening sensitively against the sheet as though his hand had touched her. 'Especially as you are my guest.'

'I can't believe...' Shaken, she moistened dry lips by biting hard.

'That a leopard can so quickly change its spots?' he suggested swiftly.

'I was merely going to say something about a change of tune,' she rebuked him. 'It is only a few short days ago that you were advising me to leave the country.'

'It is not always a woman's prerogative to change her mind,' he countered smoothly, 'and I am not suggesting you should stay indefinitely. For some weeks perhaps, so that you might get to know your nephew. As you are my sister-in-law's cousin it might seem remarkably strange if we continued to address each other formally. Have you not observed how I have begun calling you Eve?'

She deliberately ignored his last remark, sure that he

wasn't a man to worry in the least as to his friends' opinions. 'I'm sure you would survive such a contingency,' she said sharply, in no way reassured by his suave explanation. 'Besides,' she added slowly, her hesitation not unmixed with alarm, 'I am not free to stay even if I wished to. At least,' she amended, 'not until the end of the month.'

He viewed such ambiguity with raised eyebrows and Eve felt the colour which flooded her cheeks guiltily and put a hasty hand up to hide it, her eyes lowered swiftly rather than meet his.

'You don't have to explain,' he said severely. 'You see, I went to the hotel myself last night, after I had made sure you would be no more trouble until this morning, and I talked with one of the staff before consulting the good Mrs Wood.'

'Mrs Wood . . . !' Shock hit Eve hard and she could only stare speechlessly.

'Yes,' his reply came bluntly, 'but, as I have just said, before she appeared I spoke to her secretary, who was not reluctant to answer a few questions.'

'You mean you tricked her into discussing my private affairs!' Acutely miserable, Eve stared at him, her fears not proving groundless when he came swiftly upright, resorting to his old savagery as he attacked her curtly.

'Did you seek to humiliate me by working like a slut in that establishment!'

His hard words stung and hurt and started the pain in her head again, but if her cheeks paled dramatically he was not, at that moment, disposed to notice. 'You're being quite ridiculous!' she gasped, her own temper rising. 'I won't stay here to be insulted. I am not—what you just called me!'

'I wonder!' His eyes narrowed on her curved and generous mouth. He might easily have said 'you kissed like one', and Eve felt herself go hot and cold by turns as she thought she read his mind. Then suddenly his speculative glance was veiled as if he deliberately restrained himself and he briefly inclined his head. 'I apologise, Mademoiselle Eve. But why did you do it? *Tiens*,' he exclaimed, 'that room! Was it money?'

'No, no. Of course not!' In her haste to convince him she used too much emphasis which was her downfall.

'Oh, but of course!' His wits were sharper than hers. 'Didn't I hear you say yourself a student has often no money for clothes? The secretary said it was merely your second position. You did not have any money!'

'I stayed for the experience . . .'

'Do not be so stubborn,' he advised softly. 'You cannot hope to hoodwink me so easily. You wished to leave at the end of last week, I was told, but Mrs Wood forced you to stay on. That room where you were expected to sleep! A barren square, with a box-like window. And all those hordes of demanding children! Small wonder you are suffering from exhaustion. If nothing else I was satisfied that it confirmed my initial diagnosis.'

'And lost me my job! You don't understand,' she cried, 'it could be some time before I find another.' The mental picture of him sweeping ruthlessly through Mrs Wood's hotel was enough to make Eve gaze at him in horror as she visualised all sorts of repercussions. 'I think you have been impertinent, *monsieur*!'

'If so, it was only for your own good,' he contradicted. 'It would appear, Eve, you were so determined to see your nephew that you were willing to put up with any inconvenience. Such self-sacrifice should not go unrewarded.'

Eve's fingers clenched into damp palms. 'Just what did you have in mind?' she asked stormily, not unaware of a certain suaveness in his tones. Her stomach muscles went tense with nervous suspicion. Why was he so devious?

He considered her for one long unhurried moment before rising abruptly to his feet, as if her fluctuating colour and heightening tension warned him that she hadn't yet fully recovered her strength. 'There is nothing, I must repeat, for you to worry about any more. I have seen Mrs Wood and

70

arranged everything. You will not be returning to the hotel; she has no further use for you and your salary will be paid until the end of the month. Marie has already unpacked your belongings which the good secretary kindly collected from your room, and I shouldn't advise you to quarrel with such arrangements. Now, all you have to do is to forget the whole business and rest. Maybe tomorrow, if you feel up to it, we can select an itinerary which might please you for the remainder of your stay.'

Afterwards Eve blamed Raoul DuBare entirely for her continued exhaustion, the peculiar lethargy which she didn't seem able to shake off until next morning when she woke to find she had indeed slept the clock around, starting from after the light lunch which she hadn't found possible to eat the previous day. This morning, however, she felt better, really better, and though a little hazy about the time, was able to appreciate that her head no longer ached and the curious inertia she had known had almost left her.

She lay for a moment, pleasantly drowsy, subconsciously unwilling to allow the events of the last weeks to intrude on her aura of blissful unawareness. Then, with a reluctant sigh, she jerked herself back to reality and swiftly left the bed, running to the window. Below her lay the gardens, and she gazed on to green lawns and cool arbours, to wide borders, gay with flowers. Through a thick hedge of trees she thought she could glimpse blue water which might be a swimming pool, secluded and pleasant within the cool shadows of the high-walled boundaries. Although beyond this she could also see a narrow stretch of the arid, scrub-covered terrain she was coming to know, the immediate grounds were luxuriant, advertising no shortage of money, but rather a plentiful supply of it. How Carol must have loved it here, with such a beautiful house and numerous willing servants to look after her ... Remembering the mistake she had made, if inadvertently, on her first visit, in thinking that Carol had been forced to live in other, not so palatable accommodation, Eve went almost hot with embarrassment.

Unhappily confused, Eve turned back to her bedroom, and recalling what Raoul had said about collecting her clothes she went to the wardrobe and found her dressing-gown. It was old and shabby and didn't really complement Céleste's glamorous nightdress, but this latter she meant to discard as soon as she had washed. Her face flushing slightly, she regarded the short row of her clothes which Marie had arranged neatly at one end of the commodious wardrobe. The cotton dresses, most of which had been run up quickly on a borrowed sewing machine in her digs, hung limply, without either cut or notable style, something which had never worried Eve unduly until now. Frowning slightly, she turned aside, choosing instead a pair of old jeans and a casual shirt that she had worn around London on her free weekends. If Raoul DuBare found her shabbiness not to his liking perhaps he wouldn't be long in packing her off home, and while such a thought should have cheered, it brought with it only a surprising touch of depression.

Making the most of the limited time she suspected she had at her disposal, Eve opened a door opposite that which she knew led out on to the corridor and found a bathroom, complete with bath and shower. Quickly she slipped out of her dressing gown and turned on the shower, glancing wistfully towards the bath, imagining the pleasure of a long luxurious soak in water scented from one of the range of exquisite-looking toiletries which lined a glass shelf on the mirrored wall. Who had chosen them? she wondered. Had it been Céleste, or had someone else left them there? Some woman, perhaps, one whom the master of the house knew intimately? Someone with elegance and beauty, sophisticated enough to make full use of the superb, expensive perfumes to be found in those wonderful glass-stoppered bottles.

Nervelessly held, she stared through the sparkling rivulets of water which soaked her hair and shoulders before running over her slim body, the trend of her thoughts suddenly tightening her skin painfully, darkening her blue eyes. Why did she have to think of Raoul DuBare like this, a man who clearly only considered her a nuisance? It didn't seem possible, and her mind shied away from admitting it, that she had never felt the same since he had kissed her. His cruel treatment of her had, she assured herself, increased in no small way the hatred already in her heart. Why then did the thought of him with other women bring such sharply exquisite pain?

Flinching instinctively as if from a physical blow, Eve, in a desperate effort to thrust him from her mind, grabbed a thick towel and dried herself ruthlessly as she sought to regain a slipping composure. She was twenty-two, time she grew up a little and learnt to take men like Raoul DuBare in her stride—not to act like some lovesick participant in some modern tragedy who, after one brief embrace, was again longing to commit herself to the arms of a man who, with his undoubted knowledge of such matters knew all too easily how to arouse a passionate response. It was all a matter of simple experience, she decided bitterly, firmly closing the bathroom door.

She was dressed and busy tidying her room when Marie arrived.

'*Ah, bon, mademoiselle,*' she exclaimed, smiling at the sight of Eve's much improved appearance. 'You look better, there is now colour in your cheeks. You slept and slept and I was afraid you would not wake up, but Monsieur Raoul assured me you would, all in good time.'

'I feel a fraud,' Eve smiled ruefully as she thanked Marie for looking after her, and Marie glanced at her as if pleasantly surprised, as though she wasn't too used to appreciation from many of their visitors. 'Mademoiselle is too kind,' she murmured.

Mademoiselle could go down for lunch, Marie continued,

but only if she felt recovered enough to do so. Otherwise she could have it here, in her room.

Reluctant to cause any more inconvenience, Eve drew a deep breath and replied that she would go down, but first she must see Mademoiselle Céleste.

Suddenly Eve knew this was imperative before she met Raoul again. She must get things straight. It had been Céleste, in the first place, who had insisted she came here, and it was Céleste who must tell Raoul this, otherwise he might not believe it. 'Please, if you can find her, would you tell Mademoiselle Céleste I must see her at once, Marie,' she said.

Céleste came eventually, looking sullen. 'What a fuss you do make, Eve,' she grumbled, as Eve tried patiently to explain what she wanted her to do. 'Does it matter who asked you to come? After all, the main object was that Raoul should receive you. But now that this has been achieved why implicate me? He would only be furious with me!'

'But don't you understand?' Eve almost pleaded. 'He thinks I've more or less wormed my way in. I'm convinced that, although he has issued a short invitation, he secretly despises me for it.'

Céleste glanced at her, suddenly taunting. 'Surely, Eve, you are not over concerned as to what opinion my brother should have of you? Don't you think he deserves to be deceived a little after the way he has treated you? And don't you think also that you owe me a little loyalty, a little silence? After all, I have sacrificed almost two years—two most important years of my life—to your cousin's child.'

Which happened to be true in a way, Eve conceded, whichever way one looked at it. And while Eve could point out that Carol's parents had been barred from the child this had not been Céleste's fault. Perplexed, she watched, momentarily at a loss for words, as Céleste wandered to the window, pausing to tap restlessly on the narrow wooden frame before turning to face Eve again.

'You see,' she continued, her small, piquant face petulant, 'Raoul bullies me. I must obey his every command. When Dominique was alive it was not too bad, although he too must do as Raoul dictates. He must stay here and look after the ranch while Raoul enjoys himself in Paris with his *petite amie*. I have always been afraid of him, Eve, and you must remember it is I who shall have to live with him after you have gone.'

In spite of the warmth of the day Eve was conscious of chill. 'But I thought you were going to Paris almost at once?'

Céleste flipped her small hands regretfully. 'Cousin Nadine has been called to New York. Unfortunately she will be there for several weeks.'

'So it is not really necessary for me to stay?'

'Oh, but yes, it is!' Céleste exclaimed eagerly. 'She will be back—and if everything goes well here ... You understand that Mrs Wood at the hotel told Raoul you are a trained children's nanny and this has aroused his interest.'

'I see.' Eve shivered, feeling strangely colder. So it was this information which had prompted his invitation to stay, not her personally, as a woman. This of course, she hastened to assure herself, she would not want, but she hated to think she was being considered merely in the light of a possible employee. Exactly how she might be expected to fit in here as a trained nurse she had yet to work out. Apart from Céleste, Raoul surely already had adequate professional help, and only now was Eve beginning to realise how impossible it would be to stay on at the ranch by herself.

'Eve!' the girl was exclaiming loudly. 'You sent for me, post-haste, and now I am here you sit dreaming, and Raoul does so dislike being kept waiting for luncheon. I presume you are ready?' Her dark eyes swept Eve's denim trousers insolently. 'I am not sure he will appreciate what you are wearing, *chérie*.'

'I'm quite sure he will never notice,' Eve retorted coolly,

rising quickly to her feet, unwilling to explain the precarious state of her finances, wondering, at the same time, why she should allow these DuBares to hurt her so. 'I will at least remain a little while,' she agreed reluctantly, 'but I refuse to make any promises.'

As it happened, Raoul did not arrive for lunch. Marie explained that he had been called unexpectedly to the other side of the ranch and would eat with his men. 'Always there is something,' she grumbled, as she served the delicious light meal. 'Always these *gardians* imagine he can solve every problem.'

'They are busy with the herds,' Céleste supplied further details without apparent interest as she greedily attacked her lobster. 'They are checking the calves before branding. Dominique used to let Jules, our chief *gardian*, get on with it, but Raoul must go himself and see.'

Had Carol taken any part in this intriguing activity outside the house, out on the wide open spaces of the marshland? Eve wondered, knowing herself, even after such a short time, to be full of an eager curiosity regarding the workings of the ranch. Perhaps Carol had learnt to ride and acquaint herself with the herds of black bulls and wild horses, but glancing tentatively at Céleste's absorbed face she was aware that this was not the moment to ask.

Afterwards Céleste left to visit friends. 'Michel has his meals in the nursery and will now be having his rest, but I suppose you might visit him later,' she said before she went, but not apparently feeling any necessity to take Eve there herself.

Finding there was no one around after Céleste had gone, Eve resisted the temptation to seek Michel out right away, wandering instead into the garden. For the first time since she had come to France she felt lonely, strangely shut out from this wildly primitive area of the Camargue. Or was it that she still felt a little tired, and would have been wiser to have retraced her steps and gone to her room? Only if she was really well could she ever hope to take all this in her stride. Yet, after sleeping for so long the previous day, another siesta didn't really appeal and, in spite of the increasing warmth of the sun, she continued to explore the gardens, her pale face soon glowing with mounting interest in all she found there.

CHAPTER FIVE

THE gardens, Eve found, were beautiful, even more so than they had appeared to be from her bedroom window and she spent a pleasant hour walking around them. Yet in spite of her pleasure a sense of frustration prevailed, as there were so many plants and birds she didn't recognise. There were wrens, a robin and goldfinch, but she found it impossible to name many more. Among the plants there were those which she had seen in English gardens, but, as with the birds, there were a lot she didn't know. She made a mental note to ask Céleste about them when she returned.

As she had suspected, there was a swimming pool hidden away in the walled part of the garden, but it was with some difficulty that she found the narrow door which led to it. It wasn't locked and once through it she halted in some amazement. The pool was long and wide and paved inside and outside with translucent blue tiles which reflected the colour of the water and changed with every faint ripple on the surface to a shimmering, iridescent green. On the opposite side of the pool to where she stood there were changing rooms, and outside these, placed at intervals on the tiles, were numerous chairs and small tables.

Quite a place, Eve decided, recovering her breath sufficiently to wander to one of the chairs and sit down. She felt suddenly tired and glanced with unconcealed longing at one of the comfortable garden loungers, but to stretch out on it might give the impression, if anyone caught her, that she was making herself too much at home. Resisting the temptation, she stayed where she was, but the heat of the sun and soft wind which moved through the branches of the nearby trees had an hypnotic effect, and she was almost asleep again when Raoul DuBare found her.

Startled, Eve jerked herself upright. Must he make a habit of approaching her on silent feet? She hadn't heard a thing—it had only been instinctively that she had known he was there. Like a reflex her pulse had suddenly quickened, warning her in a peculiar, unpredictable way. If there was a single thought in her head it was one of relief that he hadn't found her in a more indolent position. Blinking uncertainly from drowsy blue eyes, she looked up at him as for a moment he towered over her before dropping negligently to the seat opposite.

'I wondered if I should find you here,' was all he said.

The brevity of his greeting aroused odd feelings of guilt. 'I'm sorry,' she began, 'I'm probably trespassing.'

Rather abruptly he shook his head, as if impatient with such a suggestion. 'Marie thought you were in the garden, and if you like it here by all means stay, but I think you would have been better advised to have gone to your room for a proper siesta. You are still looking too fragile, *mademoiselle*.'

'I'm quite fit, really,' she protested, with an effort speaking lightly, his voice with its momentarily caressing note affecting her strangely.

'You must take it easy for several days,' he persisted, as if she had never spoken. 'If you don't wish to remain in your bed you can come out here. Eventually a short dip in the pool would do you nothing but good. It would bring back— what is it you say in your country?—the roses to your cheeks.'

'Thank you,' she murmured, trying to remove her gaze from his darkly handsome face, unable because of a peculiar constriction in her throat to reply in any other way. 'Céleste went out,' she managed eventually, as he continued to examine her cheeks in lazy silence, 'but I haven't been lonely, *monsieur*. I have enjoyed your garden.'

'It is pleasant,' he acknowledged.

She persevered. 'This swimming pool . . .?'

'My father built it, several years ago,' he enlightened her

idly, 'when I was a boy. Dominique enjoyed it and so did Carol occasionally.'

It surprised Eve that his words brought more pleasure than pain. It was comforting to know Carol had been happy here, and she felt curiously disinclined to challenge Raoul about it at this moment.

'Yes,' she nodded, 'Carol would. I enjoy swimming myself. So does Céleste.'

'Why do you always bring Céleste between us, *mademoiselle*? Do you regard her as some kind of protection?'

Eve stiffened, the brightness of the day suddenly fading before the returning mockery in his tone. Rising to her feet, she moved with swift agitation, a slender shape against the sun-flecked water. 'You enjoy teasing me, I think. To begin with, it seemed, you wished only to dispose of me by fair means or foul. Now——' she hesitated, her face flushing with confusion, at some loss to describe accurately the way he chose to treat her now. The thread of gentleness alarmed rather than reassured, the transition from cool enmity too sudden to ring true. This outward show of benign civility could be part of a deliberate course of action, planned deviously to succeed where brute strength had failed in ridding himself once and for all of Carol's family. This man, she realised despairingly, would always be one step ahead. It was up to her to be wary, not to allow a few soft words to weaken her defences, yet how could she accuse him of duplicity on the evidence of the past two days? The flush of embarrassment in her cheeks deepened as, unable to find the right words to continue, she began to walk quickly away.

'*Mademoiselle!*' His voice caught her like an arrowhead between the shoulders, bringing her headlong flight to an abrupt halt. 'Come back at once,' he ordered, and she didn't know how a man's tones could carry such command yet be so low.

Curiously unable to follow her own inclinations to disobey, she found herself doing as she was told, even to resuming her seat, aware, as she did so, of his downward glance of satisfaction. The glint in his eyes sharpened. 'Do you always leave your sentences unfinished, Eve, or was it simply that you wished to spare my feelings? I shouldn't have thought you lacking in courage, whatever else.'

'I promise you won't find that, *monsieur*,' she retorted shortly, seeking to convince him of a virtue she was not sure she possessed, but unwilling he should guess. 'I'm sure your feelings are too tough to be dented by any words of mine. I'm not sure why I felt a desire to leave the garden, nor why I changed my mind and didn't do so.'

His hard mouth quirked, as if he understood that her little explanation was quite ridiculous. 'I am used to being obeyed, Eve,' he purred, taking her acquiescence wholly for granted. 'You will find it easier to remember.'

'Not so painful, you mean?' She had never intended referring to an incident she fancied would have been better forgotten, if only for her dignity's sake, but impulsively it had slipped out.

'So . . .?' his eyes raked her. 'Explain yourself, *mademoiselle*.'

The blood beat hot in her temples, even to think of it, and her tongue felt paralysed, but afraid that he should notice even a twinge of apprehension, she lifted her chin defiantly. How dared he pretend she had no cause for complaint! 'On my first visit here you must remember how you almost threw me down those steps? I was hurt—bruised!'

In a second as his gaze met hers it sharpened to a frown. 'You were? I didn't realise. But,' he shrugged sardonically, 'I do recall that I was furious.'

'You were that all right!'

'Hush, *mademoiselle*,' coolly restrictive, his eyes slid over her, 'you are too sensitive, and perhaps this makes you too responsive. There is a fragility about you which might arouse a devil in a man. To a small degree I still consider my behaviour was excusable, but I am not a brute. I am sure I didn't deal too harshly. These bruises you speak of?'

'I still have them faintly.' Carried away by a consuming flare of indignation, Eve pushed up her sleeve to where the smooth young skin of her upper arm still showed a shadowed mark.

His eyes dwelt on the bare skin thoughtfully, and though he murmured softly that he was sorry, Eve sensed instinctively that he was no such thing. That the infliction of pain, in her case, was something he had enjoyed, and might still do, should the need for further chastisement arise. From a distance she heard him add, 'It appears I owe you an apology, Eve.'

Her breath curiously uneven, Eve dropped the subject as if it burnt. 'I believe so—yes, but I would much rather have a few straight answers, *monsieur*.'

'To what?' His dark brows rose.

'Regarding the way you treat my family, for a start.'

'And I suggest, Eve,' he objected suavely, 'that we leave such a discussion for the time being.' As she sought to protest his hand went out to cover her nervous fingers firmly, giving emphasis to his next words. 'I can't think any useful purpose would be served by dissecting the past until we know each other better. On our future relationship so much could depend, so you must have patience, *mademoiselle*. If you are to stay here for a week or two then it is possible to leave things as they are at present. If I have been over-hasty about certain matters then I do not wish to make the same mistake again.'

So he admitted he had been wrong, but like a tyrant was not prepared to dwell on his misdeeds! Swiftly, as if stung, Eve jerked her hand from under his, a release for her taut senses. How conveniently he wrapped up years of irrational behaviour like a bundle of scrap to be thrown lightly aside, the riddles he talked merely a means of setting up a camouflaging confusion. Bitterly she stared at him, at his dark face, knowing a desire, stronger than any she had ever known before, to hurt. Yet, even as she stared, there washed over her a finely ground frustration. How could she ever hope to wound anyone so impervious? For all his plausible words he left her in no doubt he held the whip hand. If she were to protest too much, make too much fuss then, just as easily as he had given it, he could withdraw his invitation, and she had yet to meet Carol's baby.

'As you like, *monsieur*,' she agreed aloofly, her coolness giving, she hoped, a clear indication that while she was being forced to ignore the past it was not so easily forgotten. 'And,' she added, with unwonted sharpness, 'as my time is limited, I should like to meet Michel as soon as it can be arranged.'

If she had expected to annoy him a little with this last observation she was doomed to disappointment. He looked merely amused by the outrage in her eyes. 'I do believe I like you better when you forget to be the demure nursemaid, my dear. Too much sweetness can be cloying. On occasion you have a refreshing tartness which I enjoy. Carol could never defend herself as you do.'

Should he not have said Carol was no fighter? If Carol had been fond of having her own way she had usually succeeded in getting it by other means. Yet what right had Raoul DuBare to sound so critical? Active dislike against the man stirred. 'You forget, *monsieur*, Carol and I were only cousins, and she was always gentle.'

'Of course,' there was in his voice an unfeeling restraint as he rose to his feet, drawing her up with him. 'You wish to see the child? I will take you to him myself, but as you are still too thin and pale I do not want you to wear yourself out—not again. You may stay with him for a short while and then go to your room and rest. Tomorrow, if you wish, a little longer, but only in easy stages, *mademoiselle*.'

Restlessly, Eve flinched, reluctant to agree he could be right, that it was possible. Her breathing still came painfully, even her pulse behaved erratically, too aware of his steely fingers beneath her arm as he led her from the garden. She was also aware of an increasing need to oppose him. 'I promise not to do anything foolish, but I cannot rest for ever, *monsieur*.'

Eve had often wondered exactly how she would feel about Carol's baby, should she ever get to know him. Her present work would have been impossible had she not been fond of children en masse, and the one individual child whom she had looked after in her first job had presented no problems. He had been a particularly placid boy, very easy to manage. For Michel she hadn't expected to feel any immediate attachment such as a grandparent or real aunt might have done, and she was surprised at the way her heart went out to him when she and Raoul entered the nursery and found him weeping. His whimpering cries could in fact be heard as they walked along the wide corridor towards his room, and Eve was quick to note the dark frown on Raoul's face as the cries rose in volumes of sheer rage, a crescendo that subsided pathetically to defeated, hiccuping sobs.

'*Mon dieu*,' he breathed, pulling open the closed door, 'can there be no competence anywhere when my back is turned?' His voice rose angrily as, after one comprehensive glance over Eve's head, he stepped back into the corridor. 'Marie!' he called, his mouth grim.

It was within seconds of Eve scooping the baby up that a rather scared young girl came running along the passage. 'I am sorry, Monsieur DuBare,' she gasped, breathlessly, 'but Marie is too busy—*le diner, vous comprenez, monsieur? And* I must help with the preparation which she tells me is more important than *le petit*.'

'Nonsense,' Raoul declared curtly, glaring at the girl, 'You may go and tell Marie that the child is more important than any meal! I will be down to have a word with her immediately.'

'*Bien sûr, monsieur*,' the girl bobbed, Eve thought ridiculously, as she backed frantically from the room, her small face nervously reflecting her alarmed reaction. 'I will tell her, *monsieur*,' she cried earnestly as she disappeared.

Still furious, Raoul turned on Eve's disapproving stare. 'And you can take that—what-is-going-on-here? look off your face, *mademoiselle*. Michel is not neglected, it is probably a case of having too many people attending to him,' one half of whom are always supposing the other half is in the nursery, while in reality there is often no one there at all. Michel is almost two and it will do him little irreparable harm to yell a little. It is the incompetence I find irritating.'

Eve stared at him stoically as Michel clung to her like a limpet, not wholly aware yet that she was a stranger, indifferent, it seemed, to anything but the comfort of her rescuing arms. 'I haven't had time to wonder anything of the sort, *monsieur*,' she replied stiffly, as she held the baby close. 'Michel, as you say, is almost two, but a young child can suffer perhaps even more than a baby from too great a mixture of affection and neglect. Children of any age need to feel secure.'

'And I do not require a lecture on child psychology,' he said savagely, continuing unfairly, 'I will not have him turned into a milksop, *mademoiselle*. If he is mollycoddled too much he will never make a satisfactory *manadier*.'

Michel's cries had ceased, as if Eve's gentle authority had dispelled his fleeting fears. Possessively triumphant, she cradled him to her and across his head fearlessly met Raoul DuBare's narrowed, speculative glance. In yet another way he was no doubt telling her he would never let Michel go, but suddenly she didn't care. That he was irritated by the situation seemed clear. There might be room for optimism yet if she tread warily.

'I will stay with him, *monsieur*,' she replied, coolly ignoring his taunt. 'He appears to need changing. I am sure you can't object if I do that?'

'Just for one half hour, *mademoiselle*,' his eyes glinted darkly as he nodded briefly. 'Then, if you are not in your room, I will come and conduct you there myself.'

He would be quite capable of it, she thought, startled, as he left abruptly, after a swift word with the baby. Michel, to her surprise, had responded happily, holding out his chubby arms as though he was not in the least apprehensive of his formidable uncle. She had been further astonished when Raoul had laughed and tossed his nephew almost to the ceiling, and it had been when he had held the then gurgling child for another moment that she had noticed the resemblance, as she had seen it before. Michel was truly a DuBare.

'You like children?' Raoul asked, the next evening, as they had drinks before dinner. Céleste was not yet down, as it was still early, but Eve had been restless in her room and unable to stay there any longer.

'I would scarcely be a trained nanny did I not,' Eve answered, staring down at her drink, blaming the dullness of her reply to a lack of confidence in her appearance. How much better she could have faced Raoul DuBare if she hadn't felt so dowdy. Strangely enough, in the hotel it hadn't seemed to matter. There, when she had been on her own, the plainness of her attire had helped her to remain inconspicuous, but now she wished fervently that she had possessed a prettier dress. The one she wore this evening was, she realised unhappily, a mistake, and that might prove a kinder description than the one Raoul DuBare had in mind, judging from his expression! The dress was cotton, a stiff material which tended to crease each time she sat down, and the peculiar shade of green did nothing for her particular colouring. At best it was respectable, and tenaciously Eve tried to cling to this assurance, pushing all thought of something more glamorous, a little smarter, from her mind.

Raoul's eyes, she was well aware, were quite frankly assessing the cost of her entire wardrobe. Faintly resentful she flushed, not used to a man's close scrutiny although she knew his to be wholly objective, a mere curiosity regarding her unfashionable appearance. This she was prepared to tolerate, but not that he should speak outright. An English-man wouldn't have done, she felt sure, but Raoul was different.

'It is as well your figure is naturally good, *ma chérie*, otherwise that dress——! *Mon dieu*, where did you get it!'

She had expected a few more polite remarks regarding her career, and her eyes flew open wide with a sparkling resentment as they met his. 'I made it myself, *monsieur*,' she choked, 'before I came to France.'

'Otherwise you would have chosen something more flattering,' he quirked. 'I find it difficult to be captivated by what you have on. It is obvious, Mademoiselle Reston, that you are not skilled in the art of dressmaking.'

'I have never pretended to be,' she retorted stiffly, the indifferent tilt of her chin designed to hide a growing sensitivity to his criticism, and not willing that he should have any knowledge of her recently born desire for something nice, a longing which she hazily supposed might have been aroused, stupidly, by the sight of a few decorative jars in a bathroom. Raoul DuBare, she tried to convince herself, had nothing at all to do with it! 'Nor am I very interested,' she added coolly.

Idly he continued, rocking back on his heels, his teeth glinting white in a smoothly calculating smile, clearly doubting the truth of her brittle little statement. 'If, as you declare, you are indeed one of the family, then you must not resent a few honest remarks from one of its members. I personally prefer women to be chic, *ma chère*, but perhaps your boy-friends rank among today's young revolutionaries who do not consider it the thing to be well dressed?'

Innocently she fell into the trap, although she wasn't aware of it at the time. 'I have no special boy-friend, *monsieur*. I have devoted myself to my training.'

His eyes smouldered with a momentary satisfaction. 'And you have only just finished this?'

'No, I held one position before I came here.' She didn't

know why she felt so reluctant to give him this information about herself, unless it only seemed to make her more vulnerable.

He took a considering drink from the glass held contemplatively in his fine-boned hands. 'You look too young, *mademoiselle.*'

'I'm almost twenty-two.'

'So old? Forgive me, you look about seventeen—I find it difficult to believe you are older than Céleste. And you so happily devote yourself to other people's children, while being old enough to have a family yourself?'

His eyes added many things, while his face remained a polite mask. Stung by a sudden warm confusion, she answered ingenuously, 'One has to acquire a husband first, *monsieur.*'

'Ah, an old-fashioned girl!'

Eve squirmed, furious with herself, and even more at Raoul DuBare's sardonic tones, but she refused to be drawn further. Biting back a sharp retort, which might only have bounced off his tough exterior, she said instead, 'Your nephew is a good child, *monsieur.* I enjoy being with him.'

There was silence for a moment, and she felt annoyed by his lack of interest when he said, 'He is a good child, yes, well content with his lot, and I should like him to remain so, but I suggest we leave the nursery for the evening, *ma chère.* It is a time when babies, if they are well, should be tucked up in bed and forgotten.'

Which might be an easy matter in a place like this where there were numerous servants to keep an eye on them, she wanted to retort, but somehow dared not, some part of her still wary of this man's reactions. Yet she couldn't resist what was probably a pertinent remark. 'Some fathers only manage to see their children in the evening, *monsieur.*'

'And I should wish only to see my wife. You must allow that men can differ, *ma chère*, and pray do not begin to waste your abundant sympathy on a metamorphosed wife. If ever I acquire one I shall see to it personally that she has, at this hour, no thought left in her head for the nursery.'

A wave of indiscernible feeling swept over Eve, though she willed her face not to reflect it. 'It is possible,' she whispered stubbornly, 'she might not share your views.'

'She would soon forget such independence and become compliant, *mademoiselle*. I should soon teach her that these hours are to be enjoyed in a different way.'

Strangely Eve shuddered almost visibly as she stared down at her trembling fingers, something she seemed to be doing in his presence with increasing frequency. She suspected he deliberately set out to shock a little her so-English susceptibility. Yet surely he had some English blood himself? 'You had an English mother, had you not?' she murmured, as if talking to herself.

'My dear *mademoiselle*,' he said smoothly, obviously quite clearly following the trend of her thoughts, 'It was Dominique and Céleste who were thus blessed. Were you not aware that I am merely their half-brother, wholly and completely French?'

'So,' she choked, 'naturally you don't approve of English women. Now I begin to understand!'

'*Mademoiselle*——' he began, but didn't finish the sentence.

Eve's eyes fell before the impatient glint in his, and never before had she been so pleased to see Céleste. Yet she appreciated her presence more than her remark.

'You are looking quite hot and bothered, Eve,' she laughed. 'Don't tell me Raoul has managed to ruffle your so tenacious dignity?'

Eve's flush deepened even while she managed to smile carelessly. Céleste, dressed as elegantly as her brother, contrived to make her more conscious than ever of the plainness of her dress, and she was relieved when Raoul interrupted abruptly, relieving her of the necessity of replying. 'Where have you been all day, Céleste? You seem to forget we have a guest, one who is supposed to be your special friend.'

The girl laughed lightly. 'But you forget, Raoul, our visitor is not here solely to see me. You surely don't begrudge me the little freedom Eve's presence here allows? If you must know I've been to Marseille to see Amélie. I could,' she continued airily, 'have stayed longer. Amélie did ask me to, but I knew you would only make a fuss.'

Eve felt Céleste was somewhat surprised when he didn't, even now. He simply shrugged and inquired, 'How is she?'

'Oh, very well.' Céleste too shrugged as they all went in to dinner. 'She was so interested in *la demoiselle anglaise*.' Wickedly she grinned at Eve. 'Madame Troyat is so attached to Raoul that she must know of everyone who comes near him. I assured her, *ma chère*, she had nothing to fear from you, but already she is making up her mind to come and look you over.'

Unsure of her own reactions, Eve blinked, feeling Raoul's dark gaze on her head as she sat down, wondering why her heart should grow so cold at the mention of one Amélie Troyat. Madame, Céleste had said, which surely meant the lady was married?

'Madame Troyat is a widow,' smartly astute, Céleste enjoyed a little drama, 'but not such a very old one, *ma chère*, and she likes Raoul so much!'

'That is enough, Céleste.' Raoul spoke sharply this time. 'Amélie has always been a good friend, but haven't I told you before, it is too far to go to Marseille by yourself.'

'But I am not an infant, Raoul,' Céleste exclaimed crossly, choosing to ignore his level glance. 'Besides, when Nadine returns I shall probably go to Paris, which is much further afield.'

'You would do better to settle down and marry André,' Raoul rejoined shortly, 'as I should have insisted you did years ago.'

'You forget, Raoul, I am not yet of age, and not ready to oblige you by settling down with one so dull as André. And it is no use getting annoyed, because you can't force everyone to do as you command.'

'*Mon dieu . . . !*'

Eve continued with her dinner without being really aware of what she ate as she listened uncomfortably to the terse interchange of words. She was quick enough to realise that Céleste deliberately hinted at Raoul's attempt to force Dominique to marry one of his own countrywomen. But might Dominique not be alive today if he had obeyed. Glancing up, she met Raoul's enigmatic eyes and knew he had been about to reply in this vein, but for some reason changed his mind.

Not out of consideration of Eve Reston's feelings, surely, Eve thought with disbelieving surprise.

'Never mind,' he said, looking quickly back at his sister, 'it is clear you can't escape to Paris or anywhere else just now, so you must content yourself for a while.'

'Only for a while.' Céleste's consent was given grudgingly. 'In the meanwhile you might perhaps consider Eve as a suitable nanny for Michel, or better still, there is always the so obliging Amélie, who, if you were to ask her nicely, might be willing to be both nanny and wife.'

Why did Céleste's impertinent little speech stay with her, Eve wondered, all through the night? Even when she woke, at frequent intervals, it was still on her mind. Eve knew, from past experience, that Céleste when she chose could be absurdly indiscreet, yet Eve hadn't thought she would have dared to go so far with her brother. Raoul's reaction to Céleste's taunting observation had not been apparent. He had merely grinned, a swiftly sarcastic smile which Eve was sure had not reached his eyes, being mainly for her benefit. In another place, with other people, Eve might have thought the situation amusing, but somehow, here at the DuBare ranch, the humour of it evaded her.

Who exactly was this Madame Troyat, who Céleste declared would make such an excellent wife? It must, of course, be time Raoul married. He was about thirty-five but looked much older, with an authority and sophistication far beyond that meagre span of years. How was it, then, that the thought of him with a wife seemed strangely abhorrent? It could only be a form of pity for the girl who would eventually find herself in such a position.

It was still quite early next morning when Eve decided she could stay in bed no longer. Rather than toss and turn, even on such a well sprung mattress, she would go outside and enjoy the delightful early freshness of the gardens. Quickly she showered, putting on a fresh shirt and pair of jeans, brushing her unruly hair into some semblance of tidiness but not bothering with any make-up. She didn't, she considered, studying her glowing complexion, look as if she needed it this morning, and for the first time in days she realised she was beginning to feel really well. At her face in the mirror she grimaced wryly. So much for the lotus-like existence she had been leading! It wouldn't do to get too attached to such idle luxury, otherwise the sudden transition back to a life of toil was going to be unendurable!

Raoul surprised her by being at breakfast when she ran down. Usually, Marie had told her, he was gone long before this time.

'Do you ride, *mademoiselle*?' he asked, his gaze more approving than the evening before as it rested on her blue jeans which, though not expensive, hugged neatly the tender curves of her figure.

Confused, Eve glanced at him while making a great ado over the pouring of coffee. For some unknown reason she found it difficult to drag her eyes away from him this morning and inwardly jeered at herself that she should be surprised he looked exactly the same. Had she expected to find him changed overnight just because she had discovered he wasn't half English? But even that much had been a sort of bond, bringing with it, as it had, the comforting reassurance that he wasn't altogether alien. Now she felt she could not be sure of anything, and it didn't help that it was there in his eyes, the hard satisfaction of knowing that once again he had confounded her.

He had asked if she could ride, and already her silence was irritating him. As his dark brows rose impatiently she flushed and said swiftly. 'Yes, *monsieur*, I do, but hardly, I think, like one of your *gardians*.'

'That, *mademoiselle*, is nothing to be ashamed of. Our *gardians* are a race apart; one would not expect you to be immediately as good as they are, but you will learn. Our horses might not be quite what you are used to. I will, however, accompany you to begin with, so there is nothing to be afraid of either.'

'Thank you, *monsieur*,' she replied demurely. 'I can assure you I'm not afraid, although, as you say, your horses will almost certainly not be what I've been used to. I was taught at school, where some of the girls had their own ponies, which, alas, I could not afford, and the horse I rode there was old. A darling, of course,' her eyes, momentarily reminiscent, softened, 'but often I longed for an animal with a greater turn of speed.'

'Don't worry,' he said softly, his eyes on her small, vivid face, 'you will find that here. I promise you, *mademoiselle*, you have the ability to reach greater heights than you have ever known, if you leave it to me.'

Was it simply her nonsensical imagination that whispered that he was not merely referring to riding? Her breath caught as she felt his very personality drawing her closer. Yet it was this total reliance on him, on which he deviously insisted, that she resisted. The warm blood beating blindly in her temples, she stirred too much sugar into her coffee and was aware of his eyes viewing her unsteady hand with a glint of near satisfaction. 'Is Céleste coming with us, *monsieur*?' she asked.

'No.' Just that.

Eve had forgotten that he had accused her of using his sister like a piece of armour plating. Now Eve held on to her like a lifeline. Even so, she had no clear idea where her next question came from, as it was a subject she was striving to avoid. 'You said Céleste is only your half-sister, *monsieur*? Does that mean that Dominique was . . .'

'My half-brother also? Yes,' he supplied, as she paused uncomfortably. 'I must confess I am surprised you did not know?'

'Carol never said . . . Not that it can matter,' she added hastily.

'But now you feel, *mademoiselle*, I am a stranger?'

He had guessed, but only partly. He couldn't know how her quickening heartbeats, when he looked at her intently as he did now, proclaimed him no stranger.

'I can assure you, *mademoiselle*,' he went on, when she made no reply, 'a man is a man, no matter what his nationality. It is merely that an infusion of foreign blood can, occasionally, bring minor problems.'

'Such as Dominique's desire to marry an English girl?' she challenged, resentment returning.

'Not necessarily that, although he was convinced there must be immediate compatibility because of it.'

'And you didn't—you don't agree?'

'Not with every detail of his theorising, Eve.' Raoul's eyes considered her steadily. 'It is more, I believe, an inherent relationship with his country which might be bred into a man. Dominique's mother was English, a daughter of one of your own aristocracy, whose ideas as to how land should be managed were quite different from our own. In another part of France, perhaps, her plans might have been put to practical use, but not here in the Camargue. One has to be almost born in a district like this to understand it.'

'And she tried to instil her ideas into Dominique?'

'Exactly, and possibly naturally, but while she was alive he must listen to widely diversifying views from both her and our father, so it was not perhaps to be wondered at that he grew up as he did.'

'I didn't know him too well, *monsieur*.'

'No,' Raoul's sigh went deep as his lips compressed. 'He was, in many ways, an admirable young man, but always indecisive. He wished to manage the ranch, but invariably when I returned from Paris, I would find chaos in even the most simple of things. Then he would decide he must run the family business in Paris, but this too defeated him when it came to making decisions on his own.'

'Couldn't he have worked under you?' Eve ventured to suggest.

'Ha!' Raoul's smile was suddenly sarcastic again. 'It was here that your famous British independence came in! He wanted something more than this. At the same time he possessed a certain generosity of spirit which allowed him only to confess his own limitations. He and Carol were happiest when away on vacation, but alas, I found it difficult to be in two places at once.'

'Your business in Paris is important, *monsieur*?'

'It is,' he said briefly, 'but I now have an extremely competent manager who has little doubt that he can supervise me as well as an excellent staff. However, it is a great comfort to know the whole thing won't collapse beneath the first crisis when I am not personally on hand. The Paris business is important, Eve, but this is my life.'

Eve found herself considering all he had told her when, minutes later, they walked out into the cool morning air. The nights were still chilly, the approach of summer still slow, but as soon as the sun rose above the ground mist, sending its first probing rays across the awakening land, a pleasant warmth would be spread everywhere. Raoul had risen abruptly from the breakfast table, as if already deciding he had said too much, and had granted Eve only enough time to snatch a light jacket. He had impatiently forbidden her to go near the nursery.

'Michel can do without you this morning,' he had said firmly, adding enigmatically, 'You will probably see more

95

then enough of him in future, and he will not fade away, *mademoiselle*, should you neglect him for a few hours today.'

She had glanced at him doubtfully, then given in without further argument, even while her conscience whispered that she was not here for her own pleasure, but for the sole purpose of getting to know the child.

A trace of bitterness in Raoul DuBare's expression kept her strangely silent. His dry, indifferent tones over breakfast had not fooled her completely. She had seen it in his eyes— he had cared about his young brother, possibly as much as Carol's family had cared about her, and this could be another, perhaps the most important, reason why he felt he must rear Dominique's son on his own. The important factor was whether or not he was right.

CHAPTER SIX

BEHIND the house, away from the acres of luxuriant green-
ness of the grounds and gardens, lay, in Eve's opinion, the
real Camargue, and not having been far from the house since
she had arrived she now felt alive with a growing curiosity.
Something inside her craved to get out and see as much as
she could of the district before she left, probably for ever.

Raoul again wore a brightly coloured shirt with a broad-
brimmed hat and produced a similar one for Eve to use.
'The sun can become too hot,' he smiled, showing her how
to secure it. 'You must not risk ruining that beautiful English complexion.'

His eyes lingered for a moment, his fingers beneath her
chin tightening slightly as his gaze wandered, as if contemplatively, to her pink curved lips. Slowly he took his
hand away, but it was only when his eyes released her that
Eve could move.

'Thank you, *monsieur*,' she said, her voice a mere whisper
which he might not have heard.

Everywhere there was silence, they appeared to have the
place to themselves. Surely she remembered Céleste saying a
lot of men worked on the ranch, but when she asked Raoul
where they were, he explained that, even at this early hour,
the *gardians* had long since gone, He did show her the
bunkhouse where they lived. 'Many still live in small clay
houses with thatched roofs,' he told her. 'Traditionally these
face south-west away from the prevailing north-easterly
mistral which blows down the Rhone valley.'

Eve was relieved the men were all at work when Raoul
helped her to mount. 'It is three years since I left school,' she

confessed, rather shamefaced as the horse fidgeted and she clung rather than sat in the saddle.

This time Raoul seemed genuinely amused. 'So,' he grinned, 'we have here a hardened deceiver! It is three years since you last rode. Is that what you are trying to tell me?'

Numbly she nodded, apprehensive although she felt no actual fear, her only doubts being her ability to manage the small but mettlesome animal beneath her.

'Just relax,' he said mildly, with a quick glance at her tense face. 'You have quite a good seat, even though you may be no expert, and I am here to see you come to no harm.'

Just a few brief words, yet like a rare wine they flowed warmly through her. What sort of man was this, she wondered, who could, almost in the same breath, both frighten and enthrall, fill one with a rare sense of reassurance? She would be less than human if she failed to appreciate his kindness. It was the other side of him which made her cautious.

Surprisingly, before they had gone far, Eve realised thankfully that her old skill was returning, and she was in fact able to relax, even to the extent of hoping Raoul would be willing to answer a few questions.

'Yes, certainly,' he obliged. 'The famous white horses still exist, if their numbers have dropped considerably. Many breeders now cross the white Camargue horses with Arab strains, but that does not mean that the pure-bred Camargue horse is threatened with extinction.'

Raoul himself was riding a beautiful pure-bred Arab which he had told her he had imported from North Africa. It was much larger than the white Camargue horse she rode, which was only around fourteen hands. 'I think I like this one better,' she said shyly, reaching forward to pat its neck.

Raoul, to her surprise, was willing to expand on the subject when, after a gentle canter, they slowed to walk carefully along the side of a freshwater marsh. 'Each year,' he said lightly, 'many tourists come here hoping to catch a glimpse of the wild herds of white horses, some even hope to ride them across the wide expanses of the Rhone delta. In a way, I suppose, it is yet another instance of man's fascination with something whose origins are ancient. Once, in the north of your country, I visited your famous white Chillingham cattle, Of course our horses are more numerous, and their origins uncertain, but their traditions go back to Roman times when Julius Caesar replenished his cavalry with Camargue horses and the area was named after the Roman senator, Annius Camar, who was proconsul of this region. Since then tides of invaders have swept across this corner of Europe, all leaving something of themselves. The Romans followed the Phoenicians, to be followed centuries later by Attila the Hun with his Mongol hordes. Even today the *gardians* use a supplementary rein similar to the Mongols'. It lets the rider lead without pulling the horse's mouth, and this increases the animal's agility. Then from the nomadic Saracen and Moorish horsemen who followed the Mongols we have the iron head that tips the seven-foot pole the Camargue cowboy uses to control his cattle. It is of ancient Saracen design, a half-moon set between two sharp iron horns.'

Eve had listened, fascinated by everything he told her. Now, as he paused, she asked, unconsciously eager, 'Are there any herds of white horses actually to be seen, or are they now so rare as to be hopeless to look for?'

His eyes glinted at her heady excitement. 'If I were to tell you we are approaching one such herd now, *mademoiselle*, what would you say?'

'That I could scarcely believe it,' she breathed, her eyes daring him to tease. 'Many visitors at the hotel never succeeded in finding any.'

'Because they didn't know where to look,' he replied more soberly, 'but at this time of the year, when the foals are due, it is as well the herds prefer to hide themselves as, unless approached with caution, and with someone who knows them, they could be dangerous—the stallions, especially.'

'Yes, *monsieur*,' she said, and didn't see him smile, a little ironically, at her so meek reply.

'You said,' she persisted, anxiously smiling, 'you might know where to find some of these white horses?'

He grinned. 'As you are obviously willing to be unusually agreeable in return for such a favour, how could I refuse?'

'I'm always trying to be agreeable,' she said uncertainly, wary of something she couldn't pinpoint unless it was the slightest hint of a threat in his ambiguous voice? No matter ... What was one small step in the dark if it meant the chance of seeing the famous white horses? With a childish trust, after he had tethered their mounts, she put her hand into the one he held out and allowed him to lead her through the trees.

The tamarisk thicket ran alongside the marsh, and the thicket with a stretch of dry grass beyond was part of the grazing ground of a herd of about forty horses. 'This is one of their favourite spots,' Raoul spoke quietly, as they saw the horses in the distance. 'They can graze over several square miles, but they are most often to be found here.'

He would not allow her to approach too closely, but even through a protecting screen of branches she could see reasonably clearly. Barely conscious of Raoul DuBare standing behind her, she stared at the powerfully built beasts. It was an unforgettable experience. A few of the foals had obviously not been long born, and were making their first tentative, unsteady steps on legs far too long and spindly to support them satisfactorily.

'Soon,' Raoul told her, 'they will be strong enough and run like the wind. Until then they have always the protection of the herd.'

'But the foals are black,' Eve frowned, the glance she flashed at Raoul full of disappointment.

He nodded lazily, yet she was quick to notice the expert

surveillance in his eyes as he looked the herd over, something that convinced her that this trip today had not been entirely for the benefit of one curious English girl. Her disappointment went suddenly deeper, flickering to a slight pain, but was just as quickly forgotten as he explained that nearly all the foals were born black with a white patch on their foreheads. 'At about eight months old,' he went on, 'they lose this coat and by the time they are about four years old their colouring will have changed to pale grey, before it turns to its final white.'

'You know a lot about them—I suppose naturally, as I expect you own some of them,' she tacked on swiftly, realising that, having spent his life here, her first statement he might consider—ridiculous.

If he did he gave no indication. His eyes had gone back to the herd, as though her question had evoked no irritation, but was one he had heard many times before. 'Contrary to what many people imagine,' he said, 'today's wild horses of the Camargue are not really wild at all, neither in species or character, but because they live wild the whole year round they often go for weeks without seeing a human being. The herd you are looking at now is a family one, made up of stallions, mares and foals. On this stud farm I have about a hundred mares, on others this number varies, and we all have our own brands.'

Eve's interest was growing. Inside, she felt a nebulous, mounting excitement. The horses were grazing along the reedbeds, moving leisurely through the shallows. Across the marsh flamingoes skimmed the water, and the golden rays of the sun melted into the blueness of the surface, throwing back its reflections to the sky. Her whole body seemed, in some hitherto unknown fashion, to come alive, flooded to a new, singing awareness of this amazing land.

Not sure how to cope with this disrupting effect, she caught Raoul's arm impulsively, seeking for words to subdue such tumultuous feelings. 'Can't we go nearer?' she almost begged, her blue eyes clinging insistently to his silvery-green ones. 'You must know the horses if you own them, so surely it wouldn't be too dangerous?'

He smiled gently, his glance holding hers deliberately before he answered. 'They don't know you, *ma chère*, that is the trouble. It can take a long time, often weeks, before the horses get used to the sight and sound of someone, before they are ready to accept. There is no danger, as I told you before, if one uses a little common sense and remains at a distance. If you were to live here, now, I would bring you every morning and introduce you properly. Does not the idea appeal to you, *mademoiselle*?'

'You are teasing me again, *monsieur*,' she rebuked him, colour flushing beneath her skin because suddenly, inappropriately, what he suggested, even idly, sounded attractive. She must remember that she could neither stay, or come back to this delightful spot, and that no soft word, spoken meaninglessly should be allowed to tempt her imagination. As if stung she quickly removed her hand from his arm, and, after another swift glance at the meandering horses, turned away.

'It must be about noon,' she murmured, 'shouldn't we be getting back home? Céleste will be wondering where we are.'

His sardonic glance left her face to note the sun, directly above the umbrella pine under which they stood. He ignored her reference to Céleste, but he did nod his head. 'We must, in fact, be getting back to our two other horses, *ma chère*. The stallions often resent the presence of a strange horse, and while they have seen mine quite frequently, they do not know yours.'

Eve noticed he had no comment to make about her unfriendly withdrawal. It was almost as if he understood the complexity of the emotional bewilderment which seemed to hit her better than she. His strange green eyes beneath their thick fringe of dark lashes merely flickered, as if unable to restrain a faint hint of satisfaction—something, she fretted distractedly, she fancied she had noticed before. She tried, this time, to respond coolly. 'You have given me a great deal of pleasure this morning, *monsieur*. I shall not forget.'

'Don't worry, I know the score.' His white smile suddenly glinted devilishly. 'One of these days, *ma chère*, I shall send the account. One only hopes you will find it possible to settle.'

Why had he always to leave her with too much to think about? It could only make her dislike of him stronger to treat her this way. To mildly threaten reprisals, to pretend she was in his debt, when, apart from a reluctant and sometimes debatable, courtesy, she had had nothing from him at all. He had insisted she went with him this morning, it hadn't been anything she'd thought up herself! It was utterly absurd that he should think she ought to be positively overflowing with gratitude.

His hand on her wrist as he drew her quickly back through the tamarisk hurt slightly, and it was as if he deliberately intended it should, because when she tried to pull away his grip merely tightened, sending small spearheads of lightning through her veins. 'Stop struggling,' he ordered tersely. 'I'm simply guiding you through the marshes. Maybe it might be better to let you drown, but I am sure if I did, your so serious little face would probably haunt me for the rest of my days.'

Yet later he did take a few minutes to congratulate her on her horsemanship. 'You are really very good, *mademoiselle*. With a little more practice you will soon be an accomplished performer, a credit to us all.' His eyes had mocked her doubtful expression, yet he seemed to be watching her with a keen absorption, almost as if he was unable to make his mind up about something which faintly intrigued him.

Whatever it was, Eve knew what seemed to be a nearly physical relief when they reached the ranch. A promising novice or not, to her utter mortification she found her limbs so stiff she was scarcely able to stand. Nor did it seem to help the aloof little front she had contrived over the last hour that she should have to clutch wildly at Raoul DuBare while trying to regain some balance. 'I'm sorry, *monsieur*,' she gasped, furious with herself.

'If I were a suspicious man, *mademoiselle*,' he answered, poker-faced. 'I might begin to imagine you couldn't bear to let me go. 'But his hands held her, steadied her, and she closed her eyes abruptly against the darkly dominant charm which seemed to reach out and embrace her even while he only held her lightly to him.

When she opened them again she was rock-steady on her feet, the tremors only inside her. 'I'm sorry, *monsieur*,' she repeated, her gaze going no further than the hard cleft in his chin. 'You must know it is because I am unaccustomed to this particular form of exercise.'

'Of course, *mademoiselle*,' he agreed smoothly, as his hands fell away, 'but we will make a rider of you yet, *ma chère*.'

Swiftly he unsaddled her horse, smacking it lightly on the rump, explaining, as Eve watched it run away, 'A true Camargue horse is never stabled. In winter, when we do not use them so much, they run free in herds like the others.'

'It is a good life,' she whispered, involuntarily.

'It is,' he agreed, 'both for man and beast, but,' his eyes ran intently over her flushed cheeks, 'I think you have had enough of the great outdoors for one morning. This afternoon you must rest. You are still too fragile, *ma chère*.'

But that afternoon another visitor arrived at the Mas DuBare, as the ranch was locally known. Madame Troyat drove up in her car from Marseille shortly after lunch, and Eve saw at once that she was extremely attractive. Darkly vivacious, she immediately annexed Raoul, who had seemed inclined to linger over coffee—which was quite unusual, according to Céleste.

Amélie Troyat swept in as if she was very familiar with

the place indeed, and as she was obviously welcome it mustn't, Eve concluded, matter that she hadn't let anyone know she was coming. Céleste had said Amélie was curious about Eve, but surely this didn't justify a special visit? Amélie's eyes did flicker narrowly in Eve's direction, but apart from this one brief surveyal Raoul appeared to have all her attention.

It wasn't until some minutes later when she was settled by his side that she stared coolly back at Eve again. 'Céleste mentioned your visit, Mademoiselle Reston,' her eyes examined derisively Eve's faded denims, her slight, girlish figure. 'I must admit to being curious about poor dear Carol's family. You are merely a sort of cousin, I believe? Nevertheless, it is interesting to meet you.'

Amélie's expression said directly the opposite. She might well have declared aloud that she considered Eve a plain little nobody. Eve felt her skin prickle with a kind of subdued rage. Madame Troyat was apparently regretting that she had rushed all the way here in the heat of the day when there had actually been nothing to worry about—certainly nothing to threaten her so obvious hopes of capturing Raoul DuBare for herself.

You're welcome to him, and in you he might just get what he deserves, Eve felt like shouting, while at the same time being more than a little dismayed by the unprecedented force of her reactions. It surely didn't matter so much how Madame Troyat cared to insult her, Eve would soon be gone.

Because she was secretly ashamed of her own anger, Eve managed to smile weakly, but her resentment grew again when Raoul intervened sardonically, as though the matter was of no great concern. 'Mademoiselle Reston is merely here for a few weeks, *ma chère*, so you probably will not see much of her. She has come to visit my nephew in order to take a first-hand report of him to his grandparents in Rhodesia.'

'I see . . .' Amélie was speaking in rapid French, possibly unaware that Eve spoke the language. With a further contemptuous glance in Eve's direction, she added, 'But is all this necessary, Raoul? You have always been so against it.'

Raoul shrugged, it seemed indifferently, unashamedly, Eve decided bitterly, noting how he laid soothing fingers over Amélie's hand which reposed on his knee. 'There are extenuating circumstances, *ma chère*, these one must allow for. Carol's father is ill . . .'

Could he always manage to explain everything away so smoothly? A few seconds later, Eve managed to escape, still seething, still feeling the coolly taunting flicker of his eyes. Stumbling slightly, she had mumbled something about taking Michel to the gardens.

Céleste followed her to the nursery. 'You must not take offence at Amélie, Eve, *ma chère*. She is merely warning you off. I suppose it is natural, when, ever since her husband died, she would like Raoul.'

'She has no reason to imagine I could in any way endanger her plans,' Eve retorted stiffly, 'but perhaps it is a pity your brother gave the impression that I'm here on a long visit.'

Céleste's light laughter turned just as quickly to a frown, as she turned from a studied inspection of her face in the ornate mirror which hung on the white painted wall. 'But you will stay, Eve,' she begged, 'if Raoul asks you?'

A short while ago Eve might have given in resignedly, now she wasn't so sure. A kind of panic smote her, throwing her into a whirl of confusion, reducing her voice to a strangled whisper. 'I simply can't make any promises, Céleste. Besides, I don't really believe Raoul meant what he said. He was, more than likely, provoking Madame Troyat a little, to make her jealous, perhaps, although I can't think she would ever feel like that about me.'

'Because you imagine you are plain?' Céleste's frown turned to laughter again. 'But you are not so very plain, Eve. In fact, at times you can look quite *belle* !'

Beautiful! Eve sighed. She could never be that! 'Madame Troyat didn't appear to think so,' she said dryly, and with some spirit. 'Her expression left not a thing unsaid!'

'And that, when she knows nothing of what has been going on,' Céleste giggled gleefully, as though secretly not so enamoured with Amélie as she had made out. 'How would she react, I wonder, if I were to tell her you have been out on the marshes with Raoul since dawn? That he has shown you his precious horses, an honour he bestows on few. Not even me, this morning!'

Eve gazed at her remorsefully. 'I'm really sorry about that, Céleste. I did think about you, but Raoul gave me no chance ...' Haltingly her voice trailed off, and she didn't notice how frequently she was beginning to use his name.

Céleste had, and her glance sharpened with a flicker of complacency. 'I did not wish to accompany you, not this time,' she tacked on hastily. 'It cheered me so much to know Raoul begins to accept you. Didn't I tell you he would, *ma chère*? I can see Paris looming nearer each day!'

Eve started uneasily. Céleste was happy, full of a gay optimism, yet something was wrong. A whole lot needed carefully going into before Céleste could go to Paris or anywhere else. However, there was perhaps some elderly relation already waiting to come should Céleste really manage to get away. Some person Eve knew nothing about. She shrank from mentioning a chaperone to Céleste, well aware that the girl might only laugh, might simply point out cruelly that such a person was scarcely necessary, that people would never credit that there could be any liaison, improper or otherwise, between Eve and Raoul DuBare. Somehow Eve had expected the house to be swarming with relations. Many of the stories she had read about France seemed to imply that dozens lived under the same roof, and hadn't she heard Carol complaining about so many people being underfoot?

It was all too confusing. Eve's smooth brow wrinkled with

a fretful anxiety, and she felt her heart heavy with unknown dread, an instinctive feeling of disaster, worse than anything she had ever known.

Michel, a contented enough baby, had been playing at their feet while they talked. Now, Eve scooped him up, holding him to her as though the warmth of his small, nestling body could dispel all her fears. She made no further comment about Paris, instead she asked Céleste if she wouldn't come with them to the garden. There, she half hoped to find a way to talk to Céleste rationally, to suggest there could be problems regarding her plans in a sort of roundabout fashion.

But, as usual, Céleste had made other arrangements. 'Darling,' she cried, 'I am sorry...! I am obliged to spend an hour with Amélie, then André is arriving to take me out. He positively begged, and as it is also a chance to gain Raoul's approval how could I refuse? If Raoul thinks I am in love with André he will not mind my going to Paris because then he will be sure I shall come back. The garden will still be there another day.'

Michel was not a baby, in the proper sense of the word, any more. He was almost two, and toddling, although he seemed to prefer sitting on the floor, but this, Eve had been quick to suspect, was possibly because he spent long hours confined to the nursery where he had numerous toys but little chance to try out his legs on the highly polished surface. And while it would have been ridiculous, with all he had, to allege that he was deprived in any way, Eve also suspected it was easier for one of his many nursemaids to simply leave him to his own devices, a quick glance through the nursery door being enough to ensure that he was taking no actual harm. It was perhaps regrettable, Eve reflected, that he was too placid a child to object. Raoul was busy, and having too much to do would imagine that as Michel was quiet, all was well. Man-like, he would not understand that Michel might well benefit from a more varied routine than he had at present.

Quickly Eve gathered up a few things and carried the boy into the garden. On her way she stopped only to tell Marie where she was going. Marie, whatever her faults, always insisted on knowing where Michel was. '*Bon, mademoiselle*,' was all she said, preoccupied with her never-ending baking, but she did smile, and produced a rosy apple for '*le petit gosse*'.

Michel, Eve had discovered, loved the garden and, since she had begun taking him there, his small limbs were already growing brown. He quite often got dirty, more like a boy. Now she watched as he toddled around chasing the brightly coloured butterflies which fluttered on gauzy wings just out of reach of his chubby fingers. The air was heavy with the sweetly astringent fragrance of thyme and rosemary, the wild rosemary blossom which crowded the outer reaches of the garden, a delicate pale-blue haze against a rich green background. Eve breathed the scented air deeply. It was blossom time and everywhere the dark masses of shrubs and trees were smothered in brightly coloured flowers such as were rarely seen in the usual suburban garden at home. The profusion of colour she looked at was spectacular, and the glittering wings of the birds and insects which flitted in and out of the branches even more so. It would be so easy to become addicted to living in such colourful surroundings. By comparison London, even in May, was going to appear quite drab once she was home.

Michel, tugging urgently at her jeans, interrupted her wistful dreaming. Guiltily she picked him up, reproaching herself for neglecting him as much as his other nursemaids as she pretended to examine the bright yellow flower he had found. It was rather like a daisy, but she could tell him no more, yet it seemed a step forward that he had brought it to her so confidingly. He was just beginning to talk, and because he only spoke French, Eve occasionally found it difficult to follow his babyish ramblings. She was trying to explain to him in terms he might just possibly understand how a flower was made, while he in turn was laughing happily and doing his best to pull the bloom to pieces, when Madame Troyat arrived.

Amélie gave the impression that she was merely wandering in the garden passing the time of day, yet she seemed to walk across to them so purposefully that Eve felt an immediate twinge of apprehension at her rather exaggerated surprise.

'I had forgotten,' Amélie smiled, 'about your intention to come out here yourself. And how is your poor cousin's baby today?'

Too quickly she bent to poke at Michel with long, sharp fingers, and with a small nervous whimper he shrank back against Eve. He had been wholly absorbed with his daisy and Amélie's approach had been too abrupt. Then, to Eve's dismay, he began crying in earnest as Amélie continued to stare at him closely with darkly malicious eyes.

'One can see at a glance,' Amélie said coldly, 'that he lacks discipline—haven't I told Raoul a hundred times! Of course he agrees with me, but he is too busy, poor man, to do anything about it. A young baby needs a firm hand, but alas,' she shrugged, 'at the moment I have no authority. However, very soon this may be altered.'

With difficulty Eve bit back a sharp retort, not being able to think of one good reason for Madame Troyat's obvious antagonism. Madame Troyat's whole manner she found intensely irritating. However, she conceded grudgingly, perhaps the woman meant well? Some people always managed to make themselves appear in a bad light, while at heart they were full of good intentions. Amélie's manner was probably unfortunate, and Eve knew she could not but agree that children did need a certain amount of discipline.

'But Michel is young, yet,' was all she replied, as the baby clung tightly to her. 'He didn't expect to see you and simply received a little fright. A very young child often acts instinctively—he hasn't yet learnt to reason.'

Faintly mollified, Amélie appeared to relax, even to smile

again, this time charmingly, at Eve's anxious face. 'So I stand chastised, *mademoiselle*,' she laughed lightly. 'I quite see you and I are adults, and must not allow the whimperings of one small, spoilt child to drive us to a frenzy. I have been wondering,' she went on, 'if Raoul would not let you take Michel to live with his *grand'mère* in Rhodesia. How much more convenient for everyone this would be.'

A few weeks, even days ago, such an ally and such a proposition would have delighted Eve; now, she wasn't so sure. There was a hollow feeling inside her where a growing elation should have been. 'Monsieur DuBare would never consider such a proposal,' she said unthinkingly.

Amélie's glance narrowed keenly as though something amused her. 'Monsieur DuBare?' she repeated softly. Then, 'He can be so stubborn, that one,' Mademoiselle Reston. Michel must have his poor father's share; Céleste, the idle wretch, must have a dowry. It is as well, is it not, he is a very rich man, otherwise what would there be left for his poor wife when he takes one!'

'That is none of my business,' Eve retorted coldly, while longing to ask if it was any of Amélie's either. Yet why should the idea of Raoul being married to Amélie fill her with alarm? Amélie was an attractive widow and would undoubtedly make him an eminently suitable wife. It was not for her to bother her head about such matters.

Hazily she became aware of Amélie speaking, and that while her voice was still soft, it also seemed to hold a thread of threatening violence. 'Just make sure it continues to be none of your business, *mademoiselle*, then we shall have nothing to quarrel about! And as for taking the child with you when you depart—well, you think not, but I should advise you to wait and see!'

Startled, Eve stared as Amélie whipped around, walking off as swiftly as she had come. 'Whew!' she found herself exclaiming soundlessly. Madame Troyat was undoubtedly a force to be recognised, having no compunction when it came to issuing ultimatums, leaving Eve in no doubt as to what happened to those who stood in her way. All too clearly Amélie was determined to become Madame DuBare. Michel had stopped sobbing and scrambled from Eve's arms in almost the same instant Amélie had gone, and Eve sighed. Raoul would never part with his brother's only child, that she instinctively knew, but what sort of a childhood would Michel have if his uncle married someone like Amélie Troyat?

Several evenings later Eve came down to the garden by herself to sample the delights of the pool. The afternoon had been hot, unduly hot for the time of year, and after playing all morning with Michel, she had fallen asleep in the cool confines of her room. She had been quite annoyed with herself when she woke up and found it was quite late. She was also very stiff, as she had gone to sleep unintentionally, sitting in the armchair by the east window where she had only intended staying for a minute to escape the sun.

About to scramble into a dress for dinner, she had suddenly remembered that both Raoul and Céleste were out and she had told Marie not to cook anything hot, that she would just have a snack in the kitchen. Hastily she had put her dress back in the wardrobe before running downstairs where, to her delight, Marie had already arranged an assortment of cool salads on a tray with a bottle of wine.

It was Marie who suggested she took her meal into the garden, and had a swim. 'One of the boys will carry your tray for you, *mademoiselle*,' she said, smiling. 'You will enjoy your *diner* better when you feel cooler, you will see.'

The idea had suddenly appealed to Eve enormously. She hadn't yet swam in the pool as Céleste never seemed to be at home to accompany her and she had felt curiously reticent about using it on her own. But there would be no one around at this time of the day, no chance of Raoul discovering her unexpectedly, as he was not expected home until late.

So she allowed herself to be persuaded and, after murmuring a word of breathless thanks to Marie, rushed upstairs for her bikini and a towelling wrap. In the pool she had dived and swam until once again she was tired. Now, drowsily replete after enjoying her meal, she was ashamed to realise she could very easily go to sleep as she had done just a few hours earlier. The air was still and warm, the shadows gathering as the light began to fade. Even the piercing cries of the birds had dropped to a murmurous twittering, and the last busy insect retired for the night. Soon she would have to retire as well, but right now she couldn't seem to manage the effort to move. Her recliner was the last word in comfort, padded softly with cushions and boasting a huge fringed umbrella overhead. Idly Eve wriggled bare toes, while scarcely conscious of any movement at all, only aware it was a long time since she had felt so relaxed.

It was perhaps because of this, when she lifted her heavy eyelids to find Raoul DuBare gazing down at her, that she knew such an instant resentment. A twin feeling of flickering excitement she ignored, concentrating on her loss of pleasure in a losing struggle to create a sort of invisible barrier. Why must fate turn him up like this? During the last few days she had seen a lot of him, too much, in fact. Had it been totally unreasonable to hope for a breathing space? He was too swiftly decisive ever to need one, but Eve felt her own more vulnerable defences shaking. 'Good evening, *monsieur*,' she said weakly, gathering her wrap, for no reason she could think of, more tightly about her.

His eyes taunted the shaky fumbling of her fingers, his dark brows rising derisively. 'You feel a sudden chill?' he asked, his voice threaded with ironic concern.

His sarcasm hit her, scattering for ever her mood of tranquility. 'I didn't know you would be home so early,' she challenged him foolishly.

'Obviously not, but there is no need to act as though you have committed a crime in bathing in my pool. Or is it something else, Mademoiselle Eve, that disturbs you?' His eyes still mocked as his glance swung to the remains of her cold meal, the almost empty wine bottle. 'If I'd known you were celebrating, I might have joined you instead of eating by myself on the way.'

Uncomfortably Eve flushed; his teasing glance was so pointed she couldn't pretend not to understand. 'The night was hot, *monsieur*. It is only a little light wine—and I doubt,' she added, with a kind of frantic daring, 'if you dined alone.'

He laughed at her pertinent observation. 'No,' he confessed, 'I did not. At least, an old acquaintance joined me for coffee, which was not so amusing as it might have been here, with you.'

'Oh . . .' Eve's thick lashes fluttered on her hot cheeks; perhaps she had deserved that! He wasn't to know her silly query had been prompted by confusion rather than curiosity. With concentrated effort she turned her gaze away from him, attempting to find distraction in the beauty of the garden, but dismayed to find her view still blocked by Raoul's image, seemingly indelibly imprinted on her mind's eye.

As if acknowledging the hopelessness of her own endeavours, she looked nervelessly back at him, wondering rather desperately what it was about him she was fast becoming unable to resist. He might have had a busy day, there could be no doubt about that, but he still gave the appearance of being alive with a sort of devastating energy, his eyes brilliantly alert, not missing a thing. He was a man whose dynamic personality would always be one step ahead, anywhere in the world. What chance would a girl like Eve Reston have of beating him at his own game, or any game at all, come to that?

Moodily lost in a whirl of uncertainty, Eve's eyes clung to his well laundered shirt, the immaculate distinction of tailored silk. He had obviously bathed and changed since returning home, having discarded his town suit in favour of a pair of more casual slacks. He looked cool and remote, but he was, she was quite aware, all man. Very masculine, which was undoubtedly the way he was made, but he was also dangerous, this she knew only too well, and prayed silently that; while he might sway her senses, she could still retain enough coolness of head to see him objectively.

As he so obviously waited for her to finish, or to make some further comment, she said faintly, 'I don't think you would find me amusing for long, *monsieur*. As we have so little in common it is often difficult to find anything to talk about.'

CHAPTER SEVEN

IF Eve had hoped to confound him by such an obviously discouraging observation, she clearly failed dismally, as his eyes again flickered tauntingly. 'You English set great value on the lengthy conversation, do you not, my dear Eve? In France we can often think of better ways of passing the time, especially at this hour of the evening.'

Now she knew he deliberately teased, and would have liked above all things to have been able to get up and simply walk away, but it seemed as if his eyes deliberately pinned her to the soft cushions of the recliner and it was all she could manage to retain even a modicum of dignity as colour flared wildly beneath her skin. 'I am not familiar, as you know, *monsieur*, with the way a Frenchman's mind works,' she muttered crossly, 'and it can scarcely matter as I shall soon be gone.'

Without warning he dropped down beside her, on the edge of the wide recliner, facing her, his voice full of a menacing smoothness. 'The wine has perhaps made you a little reckless, *mademoiselle*. I must have a word with Marie.'

'No, please.' He was so close if she put out a hand she could touch him. 'I didn't mean to sound impertinent, *monsieur*.'

'But you do,' his mouth hardened, 'all the time. What exactly do you hope to gain by these imaginary battles you fight, or is it that you hope a lot of smoke will conceal the exact amount of the fire?'

'You talk in riddles, *monsieur*!' she cried, trying futilely to edge away from him as his hand snaked out and caught her, holding her, regardless of her brief struggle. 'Why should I have anything to conceal?'

'Perhaps you are right,' he shrugged, suddenly indifferent, although his hand did not leave her arm. He merely relaxed slightly the steely grip of his fingers, as if not willing yet that she should escape him. His hard glance examined her face, the satiny, rose-flushed skin, the wide, apprehensive blue eyes, before dropping consideringly over her bare graceful limbs. 'You are young, *mademoiselle*,' he sighed, 'at the moment uncommonly appealing, but, contrary to what you believe, we do have something to talk about, something we do have in common, and which I'm afraid we must discuss. I imagined this would be as opportune a moment as any.'

As Eve's apprehension deepened, he continued. 'We had a letter from my father's cousin, Nadine. She is on her way home and wishes for Céleste to go to Paris to stay with her for a while before they both return to New York.'

'I see . . .' Eve's voice grew cautious as she sensed the looming danger.

'You are surprised, *mademoiselle*, by this news?' Raoul's eyebrows rose slightly.

'In a way,' Eve flushed beneath his sceptical expression, and she added unintentionally, 'but I have always known of Céleste's desire to go there.'

'Always, *mademoiselle*?'

Eve stirred uneasily, hit by an utterly confusing conviction that they were nearing some sort of crisis, yet how could she think clearly when his fingers were shooting small flames up her arm in a wholly inexplicable way? 'I've known for a while,' she amended unhappily.

'So, Miss Reston,' he went on, acknowledging her retraction narrowly, 'we are confronted with the problem of Michel.'

'Oh, yes, *monsieur*.' For one horrible instant she had imagined him about to challenge her half-truths; instead it seemed, surprisingly, he was willing now to speak rationally of Michel's future. 'Of course,' she said eagerly, 'Céléste could not be expected to sacrifice her whole life to the child. It's as well you are prepared to be sensible.'

Something, a derisive flash of anger, flickered in the depth of his eyes. 'That could, in this case, be questionable!' he drawled enigmatically.

'I'm sorry, *monsieur*, that was unfortunate. What I meant was . . .'

'I feel sure I know very well what you meant,' he interrupted coolly. 'You imagine I will be willing to part with the child, that I will allow you to take him?'

'Not necessarily.' Eve's voice trailed off as she drew a deep breath, impatient that he could so easily confuse her, 'You might have plans of your own.' He could have decided to marry Amélie, or there could be others only too willing to oblige, especially if he was as wealthy as Amélie reckoned he was. Apart from this it was surely not impossible to find satisfactory help.

'I have plans, yes,' he was saying, pausing, watching her expressive face closely, reading clearly the muddled trend of her thoughts. 'I have known of Céleste's unrest for some time, but until you arrived a solution eluded me.'

Rather desperately Eve stared away from him. She might have known he had seen through Céleste's too elaborate contrivances, but he couldn't actually be admitting he found her ideas feasible? 'You mean . . .?' she began, with a painful hesitation.

'I mean, Eve,' he again cut in firmly, 'or rather, I am suggesting, that you knew something of my sister's attempts to enrol you as nursemaid.'

Bright colour stained Eve's cheeks and she felt guilt must be written all over her. 'There was nothing definitely arranged,' she faltered. 'My aunt and uncle were very anxious to have news of their grandson.'

'So you just came, hoping to see him, and suffered all kinds of reprisals because of it? Such devotion to one's infirm relatives ought not to go unnoticed, *ma chère*.'

But it hadn't been altogether like that! Eve felt like crying. Hadn't she only come reluctantly, resenting wildly the conscience which had seemed to drive her here? This, and the wholly alarming fear that Céleste would carry out her threats and bring Michel to London, was almost entirely responsible. She was no self-sacrificing heroine as perhaps Raoul appeared to think, yet how could she explain this without implicating Céleste? But she was in fact searching for a suitable way to confess when his next words drove all such thoughts from her head.

'I have decided, Eve, it is not merely a nurse I must look for but a wife.'

Heavens! For a moment she was startled, before the surprise inside her seemed frozen cold. 'A wife!' she whispered, paling clearly as a shiver ran through her.

'Why not?' he demanded, as she stared up at him.

'But of course, *monsieur*,' realisation dawned. 'A nurse, a young one, anyway, would require a chaperone perhaps ... Madame Troyat ...'

'Go on,' he murmured sarcastically, as she faltered, 'you were saying?'

'Oh, please,' she gave him a scared glance, 'it was only that Madame Troyat also said a wife would be the best thing. She was speaking generally—you understand? Someone who would see to it that the nurse looked after Michel well.' She dared not tell him of Madame's other plans for Michel—there was such a lot she was too frightened to tell him, his anger could be harsh.

'So,' he drawled dryly, 'I am to be saddled with both a wife and a suitable nanny, two people when it is probably only necessary to find one.'

'But Madame Troyat ...'

'We will put the good lady to one side for the moment, Eve, although she may yet be necessary. She is indeed a most admirable person, but it is you who I am asking to consider this position. I am asking you to be my wife?'

'*Monsieur*, please!' she felt herself go white. 'I don't imagine,' she gasped, 'you are serious, but I don't somehow appreciate your little joke!'

'It is no joke, *ma chère*.' His mouth curved ironically, as he looked down at her numbed face. 'Do not look so completely disbelieving. This is not an entirely new idea, something unheard-of. Men have been marrying with the same purpose in mind throughout the ages. In finding someone with your training, who suits my purpose admirably, I have been more fortunate than many others, shall we say.'

Eve had a strange feeling, as she listened to him, that she was sinking in water so deep she could never hope to reach the surface again. That she was drowning, but perhaps in oblivion she might rediscover some kind of sanity. Now, as her eyes widened on his hard, handsome face, she realised he meant each word he uttered. And yet it did not seem possible.

Unconsciously she moistened dry lips. 'Apart from my own feelings, *monsieur*,' she said, 'are you willing to sacrifice all hope of marrying someone you love in order to benefit a boy who isn't even your son?'

'Oh, I would find compensations, *mademoiselle*, never fear. There is much which might be arranged.'

'Maybe you are thinking of divorce, in a few years' time, when Michel is older?'

'A Frenchman quite often does not marry until he is older, *mademoiselle*, but when he does it is for the rest of his life, usually.'

'But . . . !' Eve's breath seemed driven from her body, and as she spoke a wild flush returned to her cheeks. 'But, if it was not a proper marriage, *monsieur*?'

His eyes were enigmatically veiled. 'One crosses all these hurdles as one comes to them, *ma chère*. There is always a solution, and not always the obvious one. At the moment, as

I think you must agree, the child is the important consideration.'

He talked in riddles, terrible, heart-accelerating riddles. 'What you suggest is of course impossible,' her voice gathered a little strength and confidence as she tried to thrust all thought of it from her. 'You could easily find a suitable nanny and some elderly relation to act as chaperone. I would myself be willing to stay on a little while longer in these circumstances.'

'Then you will leave,' he commented dryly, 'and once more the child will be at the mercy of change. And the elderly relation who is free to come, whom I could possibly endure in the house, does not exist. So you must think again, *mademoiselle.*'

'I'm sorry,' Eve replied stiffly, in no way convinced.

His broad shoulders lifted, the muscles moving smoothly beneath his thin shirt. 'So am I,' he shrugged.

Eve glanced at him apprehensively. It was merely a polite rejoinder, his tone holding no obvious regret, as though, in his opinion, in spite of what she said, a satisfactory outcome was simply a matter of time and patience. She would have liked to escape, but his hand still held her arm and he made no attempt to release her, and when he began to speak again she could only wait submissively to hear what more he had to say.

'Take a few days,' he instructed coolly, 'to think about it. Think also of the relief your uncle and aunt will know should you change your mind. Your uncle's heart, Eve, would surely benefit accordingly.'

'I don't need to think about it,' she insisted stubbornly, refusing to be blackmailed in this fashion.

He went on as if she had never spoken. 'Then perhaps if you still refuse I must ask some more obliging lady. Someone with a tender, loving heart, such as Amélie Troyat, who I suppose would look after my nephew almost as well.'

'I'm sure she could, *monsieur,*' Eve retorted sharply,

through a disquieting surge of dismay. Yet he mocked her so openly with his eyes that temper licked along her own veins so that she must retaliate. 'You are a fool, *monsieur*, to imagine a liaison between the two of us would work out. We have nothing in common!'

Hard anger flared visibly in his eyes and his fingers tightened. 'We are not incompatible.'

'That I cannot believe, *monsieur*!' Hysteria, rising from tension, rose chokingly. He did not like it when she called him a fool, she could see. It was a raw flick to his pride even if he could control his anger better than she. 'You are not only foolish,' her voice rose wildly, 'you are stupid, stupid . . .'

It was enough! He didn't attempt to disguise his contempt, the rare impatience that flickered through him at her reckless words. 'You talk too much,' he said sharply, 'it is you who is being stupid, I'm afraid. Don't you know better than to provoke a man in this fashion?'

Her fingers clenched to stop her hands from shaking. 'That wasn't my intention,' she assured him quickly, as coolly as she could, 'I was simply trying to convince you that what you have in mind would never work in a hundred years!'

'Really?' In other circumstances there might have been grim humour in his voice at such a forthright exclamation, but whatever it was it wasn't strong enough to dissolve his prevailing anger. His jaw hardened abruptly, and she felt the movement of his hands against her skin as they slid round her, behind her shoulders, almost lifting her from the recliner.

Then the warmth of her body was in his arms and he was saying roughly, 'Must you always have proof of everything? There is apparently only one way to help you make up your mind.'

Sheer, primitive alarm shot through her as she tried to pull away from him, but he merely followed up her ineffectual struggles, bending over her until she was stretched tautly against the lowered back-rest, her eyes, wide and distressed, never leaving his face. 'Don't,' she whispered, her voice a low cry in her throat, but he came right on, not stopping until he was crushing her to him, feeling the futile protest of silk and flesh under his hands and her mouth trembling piteously beneath his.

His arms held her to him with the same unrelenting strength she had known once before and there was no gentleness in his kiss, which was clearly meant as a punishment for daring to defy him. Yet the harsh shock of it evoked a bewildering response within her, something that seemed to hold her in a fearful void where all rational thought deserted her.

She wanted to push him away, but instead she clung to him, and when momentarily he lifted his head, her lips were soft and seeking against his, and the sweetness of her parted mouth seemed to loosen something in him which he could not subdue. He saw her eyes blurred with emotion and felt her hands move behind his neck, and there seemed nothing but a great silence, holding them immobile, locked together.

There was a danger around them that deepened, almost uncontrollably, and as if sensing this the man drew back slightly while Eve's head whirled and the blood pounded painfully in her ears. Quivering, she could not lift her heavy lashes to look at him, but she could feel his gaze, his breath on her hot skin, his fingers threading her tumbled hair, gripping the silky strands of it as she breathed eratically.

'*Mon dieu!*' she thought she heard his voice softly, 'but I could love you . . .'

Then his lips were on hers again, crushing them this time with a demanding question in his, an unwillingness to take no for an answer. She felt his broad shoulders pinning her down, and sensation tore along her veins, racing madly through her heartbeats, as he swiftly swept aside the belt of her loose robe, his hands brutally frank on her bikini-clad body.

When next he raised his head she wasn't so inarticulate, she did manage his name. 'Raoul,' her voice was a shaken whisper, the sureness of his touch proving an almost intolerable stimulant.

'Would you still say we are not compatible?' he persisted, drawing an audible breath as she lay quivering in his arms.

Numbly she tried to answer, to nod stubbornly, but nothing happened. There was only her heart thudding into his, and she was vaguely aware there was nothing but the silk of his shirt between them as he began kissing her passionately, his caresses hard with barely restrained desire as they recognised the urgency within her and was more than able to satisfy it. And Eve found herself only clinging and clinging.

Then suddenly he was standing some feet away from her as Céleste came running, calling, into the gardens. 'Tiens!' Eve heard him exclaim. 'Can there be no peace anywhere!'

It was almost dark, Céleste but a dimly definable figure, but Raoul turned, walking purposefully towards her—so obviously to give Eve an opportunity to adjust her robe that as reality returned, a flush of pure shame seemed to cover her completely, but when they returned together, Céleste chatting vivaciously, in Raoul's green eyes as they surveyed her still lingering distress there was not, so far as Eve could see, one flicker of sympathy—or regret!

For some time after the incident by the swimming pool Eve seemed to live only half aware of the world about her. Every sensitive part of her seemed to be steeped in a kind of agony, inducing awareness of her own weakness. Even her normal colourful energy seemed depleted, as though Raoul had, in some devious fashion, drained it away from her, and the usual daily routine with Michel was almost more than she could manage. There was a lassitude within her impossible to fight; it even seemed reflected in her appearance. Her eyes when she watched Raoul DuBare, when she thought herself unobserved, were wistful, shadowed with a puzzled confusion which held her mouth taut. It was only when she remembered his kisses that her pink lips unconsciously softened to a quivering awareness that not even a determined coolness of manner could disguise.

She couldn't seem to find any of the right answers. There were so many things to be done, yet the effort to organize her thoughts constructively brought only pain, something she fled from instinctively. There was Céleste to be informed about her return to London—a date to be definitely fixed for it. And the problem of Michel's future to be decided on, this in a way that might at least partly satisfy his grandparents in Rhodesia. Yet, as the days evolved into weeks, she came no nearer to the making of any of these apparently simple decisions. At times she thought almost frantically that it was as if Raoul stood in the background, ironically contemptuous of her obvious inability to take this last decisive step towards freedom.

She wasn't sure how much he had guessed merely by kissing her, but, if he was as knowledgeable about women as he was reputed to be, he had probably found it easy to judge how little she knew about men. Just how difficult she would find it to keep him at a distance should he really try to storm her defences she did not know? At night she could only bury her hot face in her pillows, quivering with humiliation when recalling how eagerly she had responded in his taunting arms. There was all the time the frightening conviction that he was simply watching and waiting, well aware that his experienced caresses had acted like a drug, for which, so far as Eve was concerned, there was no known antidote, no means of resistance. Nor did it do anything for the last remaining fragments of her confidence to realise it would be foolish to stay and even to try to fight a battle in which she would so obviously be the loser.

If Raoul had loved her it might have been different, but

his proposal had been accompanied by no such declaration—
Eve shuddered, recalling his businesslike tones. Why did he
want to marry her? Of course an arranged marriage, especially one directly linked up with his family, would not seem
so strange to him, the structure of French family life being
strong. More and more, during the few weeks she had lived
here, Eve was coming to realise this. Dominique's child was
part of it, and Raoul was apparently convinced that by
marrying Eve there would be no further risk of Michel being
removed from his care. On top of this there must be the
added assurance of her impeccable training, the fact that she
had already worked with a French family, all of which
would give added defence against the claims of others in
Michel's future.

Perhaps if Eve could have looked at it from the same un-
emotional point of view it could have been easier, but certain
things, she was finding, hurt too much. Amélie Troyat
seemed always to be visiting, sometimes staying overnight,
and always to be found near Raoul. Occasionally Céleste and
Eve went up to bed leaving the two of them deeply absorbed
in conversation.

'She is out to get him, that one,' Céleste giggled derisively
as they climbed the stairs. 'Do you think, Eve, she will succeed?'

'She might,' Eve managed, with commendable indifference, considering the sinking feeling in her tummy. 'Your
brother appears to be fond of her. He certainly seems to find
her company stimulating. He must at least like her a lot.'

'Oh, as to that,' Céleste shrugged carelessly, 'I should not
be at all surprised if he is at this very moment making love to
her. But as for marriage—that, I imagine would be quite
another thing!'

But would it? Eve wondered, abruptly bidding Céleste
goodnight and closing her bedroom door. Why was it whenever she thought of him married to another woman there
was only pain? Amélie must be suitable in every way, as

well as being, it was plain to see, entirely willing.

It was Amélie's attitude towards Michel that caused her the greatest doubts. Clearly Amélie had no great love for him, even though she might pretend a delightful affection when his uncle was around, but it wasn't until Eve came upon her unexpectedly again, in the gardens that she realised Amélie might actually dislike the child.

One of the young girls employed in the house, had taken him there to play, a daily routine that Eve had managed to establish, and even Marie now insisted on it when Eve wasn't there. Eve had, that morning, been out riding with François and Pierre, the two old men she had met on that momentous day beside the lagoon. Her riding had much improved and she loved to go out in the early morning, but Raoul insisted she never went alone, ordering the two old men of the *mas* to accompany her whether she liked it or not. In fact Eve found their company very agreeable as, once they got to know her, she found them very willing to talk about the Camargue, François in particular proving a veritable fund of knowledge.

Now she was back, after spending some interesting hours watching the herdsmen working with the herds of bulls. There had been a sick animal and they had had to ride out to the pastures to bring it home. The bull had not, to Eve's way of thinking, looked as if it had much the matter with it, being morosely unco-operative and complaining.

When she asked François about it he had merely laughed, eyeing her doubtful face indulgently. 'He is just like a man, *mademoiselle*, who is not ill enough to be anything but bad-tempered.'

Le maître was away that morning, the men said, so Eve had allowed herself more time than usual, not anxious for once about running into him. It was fairly easy, she had discovered, by staying in her room a little longer, to avoid him at breakfast, and by lunch she usually felt more able to face him without visible tremors.

She hurried now into the garden. Michel was getting to know her, to like her beside him. At last she was beginning to represent something in his small world—someone who would laugh with him when he felt like being silly, someone to cling to when he was hurt or felt sad. At the same time, knowing she must one day leave him, Eve was wary of making him too dependent, a fine balance which, with so young a child, was not easy to achieve.

Long before she reached him she heard him cry and momentarily she stopped in dismay before hurrying on. It didn't seem the sort of whimpering wail he usually made when he suffered a little fright. This had been a high scream of rage. Then, around the next corner, Eve drew up sharply, her whole being flooding with rage. Amélie was there, holding Michel, shaking him, screaming with temper, and the child, Eve could see, was terrified.

'Stop it—let him down!' Eve heard her own voice raised high as she reached them in a flash, almost wrenching Michel from Amélie's grasp. She didn't bother to speak in French, though knowing Amélie spoke very little English. If Amélie didn't understand what she said, Eve knew her expression could not be mistaken. 'You're despicable!' she cried, holding Michel's trembling body to her. 'Surely nothing could justify your shaking him like that!'

'He broke my necklace!' Amélie returned angrily. 'He just wouldn't let go!'

'He couldn't be expected to understand . . .'

'He is old enough!' Amélie cut in contemptuously. 'And don't pretend that in your country no child is ever chastised. My own sister is married to an Englishman and she tells me . . .'

'All right—I'm sorry, *madame*,' Eve's voice was suddenly flat, as she tried to control herself. Perhaps, as Amélie implied, she was making too much fuss. It wasn't really a crime to shake a child when it was naughty, only Michel was so young. Surely he could have been forgiven on those grounds alone?

Suddenly, as Eve stared at her in bewilderment, Amélie's rage seemed to leave her and she subsided rather lke a pricked balloon. 'I'm sorry, too,' she almost gasped, 'I know I should not have lost my temper, but I swear I did not hit him. I'm sure he is making a great deal of noise unnecessarily.'

Eve nodded numbly, there seemed nothing else she could do, but she was unable to rid herself of the suspicion that Amélie did not like the child, was not fond of any kind of children, which perhaps explained the fact that she had never had any of her own. 'I'll take him back to the nursery, *madame*,' she said, 'if you will excuse me.'

In the nursery Michel soon calmed down. Eve saw quite clearly he hadn't been actually hurt in anyway, that he had simply had a bad fright, and in a few minutes would be none the worse. Her own apprehension was something quite different. If Raoul married this woman how would Michel fare? It wasn't a new thought, but, until this morning, and this incident she had just witnessed, the full implications had never struck her forcibly. Amélie was beautiful, well bred, and, when she liked, charming. No one would ever believe she had a slightly unstable streak, that she might not be a person who should have charge of a small child. It wasn't, after all, an easy thing to ascertain. Eve herself was unwilling to misjudge her, even after witnessing two of Amélie's hysterical scenes.

'The child has been upset, Eve?'

Startled from her reverie, Eve swung around to find Raoul surveying her sombrely from the doorway. She had imagined him in Marseille, where the *gardians* had said he was going. He must have returned early. How much had he seen? It's nothing, Raoul,' she answered distractedly, glancing again at Michel's sleeping form. The heat and fright had tired him and she had put him in his small cot bed to rest. Now he slept soundly, his round face placid once more although the tear marks remained on his cheeks. 'It was nothing,' she repeated, unaware that the crumpled tear-wet state of her blouse perhaps called for something more by way of explanation.

Raoul's mouth thinned as his eyes went over her, quickly assessing her dishevelled appearance. 'Marie said Amélie had taken him to the gardens.'

This explained the absence of the girl who usually looked after him. 'I think the sun must have tired him, *monsieur*,' Eve answered, avoiding a direct reply as best she could.

His eyes dwelt on the colour which lightly stained her creamy cheeks. 'I see,' his glance was narrowly reflective. 'He appears to have been crying—perhaps he did not want to come indoors so early. A trained nurse can occasionally be too much of a disciplinarian, my dear.'

'But it wasn't like that...' she began, then stopped, words trembling on the tip of her tongue, words she could not utter. First it had been Céleste, now Amélie! Yet did she owe either of them loyalty? She thought not, but how could she change her own nature? If she was to betray them she would only feel miserable and, besides, what proof had she, and how was she to know if Raoul would believe her? 'I mean,' she stumbled bleakly, 'I was sure he had been out long enough.'

'Because he was enjoying himself with Amélie? I did not believe you would be rude to my guests. She was most upset.'

'*Monsieur* ... !'

'Yes?' his voice was darkly ironic. 'Have you not the grace to look ashamed? The expression of a sullen child does not become you.'

'You have no right to judge me,' she tried to glare straight into his curiously light eyes. 'You like to condemn me out of hand!'

His white teeth glinted though not, she thought, in amusement. 'I do not forget, Eve, you have granted me no rights whatsoever, to date. But there are others, my dear, who would not be so reluctant.'

'Someone?' she choked furiously. 'A certain lady you don't wish me to offend?'

'You could say that,' his smile was very white, amused, faintly cynical. 'But do not let it agitate you, *ma chère*. You are hot enough by all appearances without adding to your discomfort.'

Indifferently, it seemed, while she fumed, he put out his hands, drawing her to him. 'Occasionally I find you infuriating, little one, at the same time I do not like to see you like this.' His hand went, before she could move, to her hot brow, brushing back the clinging tendrils of damp hair, his fingers stilling effectively any protest she might have made if words hadn't eluded her. She saw in his face an impatient male tenderness mixed with a cool deliberation. 'Do you have to get yourself in such a state over one small child?' he muttered sardonically. 'Don't you think it's high time you began to waste some of these so intense emotions on a man?'

Her eyes deepened and darkened like the blue of the sky before night and she could only stare at the strong column of his throat, aware that by doing so she found none of the self-possession she sought, only a quivering reluctance to beg him to release her. He was undoing the top buttons of her shirt, his knuckles digging into her soft skin as he slid his hand under the stiff collar, easing it back. His fingers lingered on her smooth young back and he didn't withdraw them.

'*Ma chère*,' he spoke with low emphasis, his eyes directly on her slender young figure, 'must you always wear such exhausting, inhibiting clothes? *Mon dieu*, if you belonged to me I would burn the lot of them and buy you a few wisps of material in which you would look wholly enchanting!'

Colour swept again into her face, catching her breath sharply, making her eyes brilliant. 'But I do not!'

'Not yet . . . but I might presume it is just a matter of time before you arrive at a decision?'

'I've always told you . . .'

'I remember everything you told me, *ma chère*, but words are very rarely the whole of it.' His breath was on her cheek as his free hand touched the racing pulse at the base of her throat, his insinuation so pointed she could not pretend to misunderstand.

'How I hate you!' she cried, feeling herself a stone's throw away from total disorientation, almost unable to restrain her own arms from going up around his broad shoulders, her shaking mouth from searching for his. Desperately, puppet-like, she stared at the faint stripe in his white shirt, willing herself rigidly from doing any such thing.

His hold tightened on her, hurting for another minute before suddenly he let her go. 'You'd better go and change for lunch,' he mocked, 'if you're still determined to play it safe. Shall I see you to your room? The house is very quiet.'

'There is no one around,' the glinting devil in his eyes seemed to add, 'and, although you may pretend, I shouldn't so much as wager two cents on your resistance!'

And he could be right, Eve admitted, terrified for the first time in her life by a man's tauntingly obvious thoughts as she turned and fled.

In her room, all the time she scrubbed her hot face and searched for a clean shirt, she tried to keep her mind closed to all thoughts of him. How dared he mock her so sarcastically? He couldn't really want to marry a girl after talking to her like that! What he had said was bad enough, but that which he had implied could be even worse. Was he simply expressing, she wondered wildly, his general opinion of women, or was it just herself? Perhaps she deserved it—his apparent disrespect? He must have guessed she lingered here not merely because of Michel. Shivering with alarm and confusion, Eve thought of the way she seemed always to respond in his arms. Might he not be excused if he imagined

132

she would settle for a—less permanent relationship? It wasn't difficult to recall how hardily he had proclaimed he hadn't a drop of English blood in him. A wholly decisive man, and how little she knew of him. He would demand— no, take, more than she would be prepared to give, and daily the danger mounted. It was up to her to make the effort, to prove once and for all that she really had the strength to turn her back on him and go.

Amélie didn't come in from the gardens until Marie sounded the old-fashioned gong for lunch, merely going to the downstairs cloakroom to rinse her hands and not appearing in the dining room until everyone else was seated. It might appear she had been unwilling to confront Eve again, or had simply waited, with supreme confidence, for Raoul to annihilate her.

Eve noticed throughout the meal how Amélie's eyes gleamed spitefully as they wandered frequently from Raoul to herself, noting, with obvious satisfaction, that they rarely addressed each other. Raoul's solicitude regarding Amélie's comfort was something Amélie took so clearly for granted that, on more than one occasion with Amélie simpering at him, Eve ground her small white teeth almost audibly. Pain stabbed and she flinched while perversely glad of it, hiding as it did a worse type of hurt, and a flicker of jealousy which, of course, she disowned.

Altogether, Eve was glad when it was over and she was able to excuse herself. The men had told her when she had left them that morning they were breaking in some of the young stallions later in the day, and she did not want to miss such a sight. Not that she particularly cared for the idea of wild horses being tamed in this fashion, but she supposed it was necessary for the good of the herds. The herdsmen, she knew, were superb, and would never treat an animal cruelly. Women, she supposed bitterly, remembering Raoul Du-Bare's treatment of herself, would be quite another thing!

She lingered with Michel until almost four, then, leaving

him playing happily with his two young nursemaids, she ran down to the sheds where the *gardians* were already busy. Eagerly Eve climbed on to the top of some high wooden railings to watch. Young stallions of about three to four years old were caught in the marshes and brought back to the *manade* where they were handled to get them used to people before being ridden for the first time. It was hard work, sometimes dangerous, as the animals seemed instinctively to know they would never again have the same freedom and rebelled accordingly, their hooves flying out wildly at anyone who got in their way.

The mistral had been blowing for several days now, and it was hot and dusty, but Eve didn't care. The dust was the worst part of it, clinging as it did to her clothes and hair, getting in her eyes, half blinding her. Yet somehow the discomfort went unnoticed, surrounded as she was by numbers of excited horses, and equally excited men. Horses are creatures of habit. They liked familiar, well worn tracks, known grazing grounds, a regular pattern of activity, and object when this pattern is broken. All this Raoul DuBare had explained to *her* on one of the rare occasions when he had taken her out—excursions to be treasured but not dwelt on too deeply. Exactly how an animals instinct works was still a mystery, he'd said, but a horse's perception was infinitely more sensitive than man's. In thick darkness a horse could find its way home without any difficulty, while anything new or different on its path would immediately arouse its suspicions.

François, Eve's faithful shadow, was giving a running commentary on the proceedings, encouraged perhaps by her animated expression. She listened fitfully, her whole attention diverted when one of the herdsmen, riding a working horse, brought out a young, unbroken stallion on a leading-rein. She watched closely as the man worked carefully to get the wild horse used to the saddle, holding her breath almost painfully as the horse reared, trying to get free.

'You are interested, *mademoiselle*?' At first she absently assumed it was François who had spoken, until the different timbre of voice broke through her absorption. She didn't need to turn to see who was standing behind her. Her pulse leapt even while she kept her eyes fixed steadily in front of her. Fervently she had hoped he wouldn't be here and, for a short time, she had felt completely relaxed because he wasn't, but she might have known he would arrive.

'Why, *monsieur*,' she heard herself saying blankly, 'You seem bent on startling me today . . .'

CHAPTER EIGHT

IMMEDIATELY she had spoken Eve flushed. That sounded naïve, but did his brows have to shoot up so sarcastically? She let out a faintly stifled breath that had nothing to do with the dust, aware that he waited for some kind of explanation. 'I had nothing planned, *monsieur*,' her voice faltered. 'I came on impulse.'

If anything his brows rose higher. 'You don't have to make it up as you go along, child,' he rebuked ironically, 'spare me that! If you had mentioned that you wished to come here today I would have brought you myself.'

Eve gulped, fixing an unfocused look on a point somewhere beyond his shoulder. 'I cannot tell you everything, *monsieur*, we are not on those kind of terms. Besides, you were talking with Madame Troyat, so I imagined you had other plans for the afternoon.'

He ignored this, but his mouth tightened at the corners as he looked at her. 'Why can't you be your age! Must you always act like some crazy child, sitting in the dust as if it was sand on the beach! What you really need is discipline, and one of these days, when my patience is at an end . . .'

His voice was low, and Eve did not need to glance at him again to know he was furious. Recklessly indignant, she retaliated, 'You sound just like a disapproving parent, *monsieur*.'

'A while ago it was Raoul!'

Her lashes flickered. this time uncertainly. 'Only because you startled me.'

'Now you choose not even to look at me!' As if conscious of other ears listening, he spoke in savage undertones, something about her obviously driving him beyond sufferance.

Surely her lack of elegance should not offend him to this extent? Eve's blue eyes clouded curiously as, as if compelled by his anger, they turned apprehensively back to him, her glance clinging with a sudden, startled surprise to his checked shirt. She hadn't noticed he was dressed like one of his own men, and obviously not for pleasure. It couldn't be that he intended riding one of those snorting, infuriated animals himself?

'Eve!'

As her expression grew trance-like with dismay, his sharp tones jerked her upright. 'I'm sorry,' she gasped, her voice containing now only the shadow of a shaky defiance, 'But I am looking at you as you requested, *monsieur*, if it was necessary?'

'*Mon dieu!*' he countered, missing completely the fears which beset her, in his apparent desire to shake the life from her. 'You parade in front of my men in a pair of jeans so tight they leave nothing to the imagination! You sit on a fence like a young boy, not caring what the dust and dirt does to your skin! If you were mine, *mademoiselle*——'

'But I am not!' Eve cut in, feeling it was a point to be immediately emphasised, her heart thumping again at his sheer male arrogance.

'Not yet!'

'*Monsieur ...?*' His chief *gardian* approached him, seeking advice, and Raoul turned abruptly from Eve, dropping her arm, though not his dark scowl, and she stared after him compulsively, every nerve end tingling as if with shock, as he walked towards the horses.

'Stay there and don't move until I am finished,' he commanded curtly, obviously indifferent as to whether the men heard or not. 'I will not be long, then we shall return to the house.'

Mutinously numb, Eve gazed after his tall, dark figure. He towered way and above most of his men and was also much heavier built, although he moved with a litheness which matched even the youngest of them, and was clearly, in every way, supremely fit. Unconsciously her fingers crept to her arm, where his hand had touched her, remembering how he had held her before lunch. It wasn't sensible to wonder if he liked the feel of her body close to his. With his hard masculinity perhaps any woman, not necessarily any particular one, would do.

In minutes his long stride took him away from her, to the other end of the huge enclosure, where she lost sight of him amidst the general mêlée of animals, dust and men.

The first horse she saw was saddled and walking quietly on the leading rein. Now it was time for someone to try and mount him, and this wasn't accomplished immediately. Eve drew in her breath sharply as she listened to the encouraging calls of the *gardians* as the first man succeeded in staying in the saddle and both horse and rider disappeared in the ensuing swirl of pounding hooves and dust. The stallion's frenzied body flashed through the air as he tried every trick to unseat the man, but the exuberant *gardian* won. It was a clash of wills, a battle of strong temperaments, the outcome foreseeable if not to be taken for granted.

It was a ritual, born of necessity, that the young stallions should be broken and learnt to tolerate the saddle, as no one in the Camargue rides a mare, these being kept for breeding. After today's session the stallions would be gently and patiently schooled until they were ready to be mounted normally. The mutual respect between the famous *gardian* and his horse was something one was instinctively aware of.

Raoul, to Eve's relief, because she wanted to stay a little longer, remained where he was, and when one of the stallions managed to throw two men he mounted it himself. Eve felt herself tremble and her hands go slack with perspiration on the rails as she watched, unable, for a moment, to conceal the depth of her fear. She had been aware of Raoul DuBare's good horsemanship, and she could see now he was superb, but it didn't stop her from shaking, from being suddenly terrified for his safety. The animal, having already triumphed over two men, was quite confident of getting rid of a third and reared and bucked with this clearly paramount on its mind. Impossible . . . ! The men laughed and cheered, relaxing after the first few traumatic seconds when it seemed that victory might almost be within reach of the infuriated horse. Eve's heart was in her mouth, which seemed uncommonly dry, when a short time later Raoul stepped down, as coolly as if he had merely been out on a leisurely excursion. *Le maître* was obviously a hero in the eyes of his men, indifferent while she had been fraught with anxiety about a danger, which for him, hadn't seemed to exist.

But the danger, it seemed, was there, not for Raoul but for herself. Another of the young horses managing to throw its rider, broke free from the lead rein, and, before anyone could move, charged wildly at the wooden fence on which Eve was perched. It all happened so swiftly she couldn't afterwards recall a thing. One minute she was sitting comfortably, gazing bitterly at Raoul DuBare, the next, she was lying flat on her back, a canopy of slashing hooves flying over her.

She couldn't be hurt, although the breath seemed to have been completely knocked from her body. Backwards she had been flung, every part of her jarred with the unhampered force of her fall, a small scream of frightened surprise echoing faintly from her lips. She hit the hard ground with a softly audible thud, and lay, momentarily unable to move, a slender, crumpled heap against the dry, arid earth, the fragments of broken railings scattered all around her.

'*Mon dieu!*' From a distance she heard Raoul's furious exclamation, and tried to open her eyes immediately so as to assure him she was only—the word stupidly eluded her— winded! It couldn't be more. At least, nothing to justify the way in which his hands were going ruthlessly over her, probing, it seemed, every bone of her body. Then he was picking her up, holding her to him with a force which she unhappily suspected might be doing more damage than her actual fall.

He was shouting to the men, his language only fit for the ears of the unconscious, so for a moment she considered it advisable to retain this appearance. He sounded like a man very near the end of his tether, but it was enough to lie limp, for once letting his anger flow unanswerably over her.

'And you,' she heard him hiss in her ear as he carried her towards the house, 'you may open your eyes. I am assured the damage is not irreparable. You deserve to hear everything I have to say for sitting on that rotten fence. *Mon dieu*, I need my head examined for allowing you to remain there, but must you always be in some kind of trouble, *mademoiselle*?'

'I'm sorry,' she whispered, her voice weak, not from the injuries he so rightly wouldn't allow her, but she had received a fright and felt badly shaken. His rotten fence, as he called it, had been quite high! All she needed was the consolation of his arms, just for a few more minutes, even if he felt no actual sympathy. His heart thudded into her through the blue and black check of his shirt, and she caught the dusty, perspiring heat from his body. Insanely she wished suddenly that the house was miles away. Her fall might have taken all her breath, but it had also seemed to remove all her resistance, leaving her trembling, unable to hide her devastating emotions. 'Oh, Raoul,' she moaned, pressing her hot face frantically against his broad chest.

'Be still,' he ordered grimly, obviously thinking her wandering in the mind. 'You could have hurt your head. *Un docteur* ...'

'No, no,' she cried, fully aware of his instant rejection, 'I don't need a doctor. You can let me down, I can walk.'

But, all at once, they were at the house, and Amélie was there, the sharpness of her glance, the suspicion in her face

140

too apparent. Eve caught her glance and there was hate in it, warring with a patent disbelief.

Amélie's laughter came shrill as she saw Raoul lowering Eve gently down to the sofa. 'Good heavens,' she exclaimed, 'whatever has Eve been up to now?'

Raoul didn't answer. He took no notice of Amélie at all as he gently swept Eve's fair hair back from her pale forehead. 'Am I to be always doing this?' he murmured enigmatically. 'Will you never learn to look after yourself?'

Eve stirred beneath the piercing scrutiny of his eyes as they searched her white face, but before she could speak, Amélie intervened again. 'Would someone mind telling me what has happened to Mademoiselle Reston? Does she have to have all your attention as well as your sympathy, Raoul?'

'She was knocked from the railings on the fence. Quite easily she might have been killed,' Raoul retorted, sharply abrupt as he went to pour brandy.

'So,' Amélie's eyes were spiteful, 'what else would you expect of one so foreign to our ways! Who would flaunt herself from such a position in front of all your men! Surely you haven't forgotten Carol?'

'That will be enough, Amélie!' Raoul's voice was rough as he thrust the brandy into Eve's hand instead of administering it himself as had obviously been his intention a moment ago. He appeared to dismiss Amélie's vindictive accusations curtly, but Eve saw from his slight frown that there was something he had indeed overlooked.

With a great effort she managed to get to her feet, welcoming Marie's timely appearance in the doorway. 'If you will excuse me, Raoul,' she said hastily, feeling slightly sick, 'I think I'll go to my room.'

Marie went with her, on Raoul's orders, while he stayed with Amélie, staring steadily down into the glass Eve had given him back and surveying the untouched contents moodily. It was nothing, Eve told herself stolidly as Marie helped her upstairs, and, if she felt hurt, she couldn't altogether blame Amélie. It was plain Raoul had been fed up with her behaviour, by what he had said as he had carried her in. This would be his way of making doubly sure she didn't attach to his small act of chivalry any of the wrong conclusions. And it was also clear that he sought to allay any suspicions Amélie might have by not bothering to escort Eve even so far as the drawing-room door.

Eve's head ached for the rest of the day, but after a good night's sleep she felt a whole lot better, apart from the persistent ache in her heart and limbs. The soreness of her limbs was only to be expected, she smiled wryly, when Marie, bringing her early morning coffee, asked how she was. Eve didn't mention the condition of her heart.

Raoul hadn't come near her again the previous evening, but had instructed Marie to bring her a light meal upstairs to save her the discomfort of coming down for dinner.

'*Le maître* is always so thoughtful!' Marie had explained, and while obviously wondering why Eve hadn't immediately agreed with her, had put down her reticence to her fall.

How could Eve possibly have told her, that for one short visit from *le maître* she would gladly have forfeited a thousand dinners! But then Marie might have understood no better than she did herself.

A few days later Raoul went to Paris, the direct sequence of a telephone call from his manager. He would be away, it seemed, overnight. 'It would seem I am not so dispensable after all,' he shrugged dryly, as he said goodbye at breakfast, before departing.

He had apparently addressed the three of them, but his eyes had lingered fractionally longer on Eve's glistening fair hair, the paleness of her cheeks as she made a great ado of stirring her sugarless coffee. 'You look as if you could do with some fresh air, *ma chère*,' he had suddenly frowned. 'I have told you before I will not have you wearing yourself out over the child!'

'Of course not, *monsieur*,' was the most she could manage,

feeling, in some peculiar way, more like weeping than wishing him a gay farewell as Céleste was doing, or getting up from the table and kissing him tenderly, as Amélie was doing.

'Nothing from you, Mademoiselle Reston?' he had teased sardonically, pausing beside her chair.

'Goodbye, *monsieur*. It might be different if you were going for two years,' she had retorted, trying desperately to match his light raillery while bright flags of colour touched her cheeks. Deliberately she had striven to show complete indifference, yet she could not bear to look at him in case he should read the true state of her feelings—her despair at the apparent pleasure he had derived from Amélie's warm caress.

Later Céleste went out and, after lunch, Amélie suggested that she and Eve visited the Etang de Vaccarès, a vast lagoon of some seventeen thousand acres which formed part of the famous Camargue nature reserve.

'You must see it,' Amélie enthused, adding sweetly, 'before you go home.'

Eve hesitated, and seeing it, Amélie rushed on, 'Didn't Raoul think you needed fresh air—to get out? And I quite agree with him, *ma chère*. Your pale face irritates him! On the lake there are flamingoes which nest in colonies on the small islands. You will love them, they are such a wonderful sight!'

In spite of Amélie's dramatic enthusiasm, Eve felt a strange, unaccountable reluctance. Yet hadn't Amélie been extremely pleasant all week, and especially this morning? So much so that Eve was convinced she had imagined Amélie disliked her. It probably wasn't possible, or fair, to judge someone on the evidence of one or two isolated incidents, and Eve had no wish to appear vindictive. No one knew better than herself that, where feelings were involved, it was all too easy to suspect the worst of others.

The idea of exploring the nature reserve, or at least some

of it, was tempting. Once, she remembered, Raoul had mentioned it. He had, in fact, promised to take her there himself, but she doubted if he would really find time. Time, for her, she knew, was running out. It might be better to take a chance with Amélie.

'But what about Michel?' she hedged uncertainly, feeling torn in two directions.

'But what about him, *ma chère*?' Amélie mocked gaily at Eve's anxious expression. 'Marie will do everything necessary—she loves the child. Besides, as it is so hot and Raoul is away, I have told her not to cook dinner, that something cool and light will do, a simple snack, so that it doesn't matter when we get back.'

Knowing she had run out of excuses, Eve agreed, joining Amélie in her small car outside. Now it had been decided, Amélie was in a hurry to be off, assuring Eve that it was unnecessary to take jackets and, as she had already arranged everything with Marie, there was no need to do anything in that direction either. As Raoul would wish, all Eve had to do was relax.

North of Arles the Rhone divides, its twin streams flowing into the sea across a broad plain. There is always something eerie about a delta. The river has lost its momentum, running sluggishly until the estuary opens and there is a clash of opposing forces as the sea challenges the crawling streams. In turn the river attacks, pushing muddy streamers into the clear, sparkling waves. Here, too, the earth is unstable, fought over by both river and sea. Mud covers the sand in varying depths, to be washed away in the next rainstorm, and dunes which are moulded one day are swept flat by the mistral the next.

West of the Petit Rhone is an area of small lakes and sand dunes, and to the north is a district of vineyards, rice fields and orchards. Here sheep are grazed on the drier pastures while the bulls and horses are reared on the marshier parts. It was the *taureaux* and horses which kept the marshes from being overgrown with the dense reeds.

Amélie, when she chose, could be an interesting companion, being remarkably well informed. As they went along she explained that the major part of the huge Etang de Vaccarès was prohibited to the general public. So, too, was the other nature reserve, Les Impériaux. Hunting was not allowed in this area, neither was fishing, except to a few professional fishermen from Les Saintes Maries de la Mer.

Raoul, she said, along with other landowners, still owned and controlled much of the area in between, and this was chiefly used for hunting and the grazing of the semi-wild bulls and horses. Although these places were not in the actual reserves they bordered them, and, because birds and animals rarely recognise boundaries, were almost as good. Indeed, in these boundary areas, where the animals were more or less used to the presence of people, it was often easier to approach them more closely.

The fresh-water marshes in particular provided nesting grounds for thousands of different birds, from the bittern to the purple heron, the water rail and many songsters. Wherever the marshes were heavily grazed by bulls the reeds were thinner, and here could be found terns and stilts along with many ducks and waders in the winter.

'But one must be careful,' Amélie laughed. 'These swamps are also ideal for our old friend the wild boar, of whom it pays to be wary.'

Amélie drove swiftly along the winding roads, and on other stretches where no roads appeared to exist at all and obviously required skilled concentration.

Eve bit her lip as she stared about her. This part of the countryside was not familiar and seemed isolated and lonely. 'You're sure you know where you're going?' She glanced at Amélie, trying to speak lightly, reluctant that the woman should suspect she was nervous.

'Of course, *ma chère*,' Amélie answered impatiently. 'My late husband, you know, was a great friend of Raoul's. He was also a keen ornithologist. When we were first married he used to drag me around these spots almost every week-end, until sometimes I could have screamed with boredom! I'm afraid I used to study the area more than the birds.'

And she had thought Amélie overflowing with enthusiasm! Eve felt more confused than ever. It didn't seem to help either, that she soon lost all sense of direction. As the sun grew hotter the small car soon seemed to resemble an oven, and she couldn't restrain an audible sigh of relief when eventually Amélie stopped.

'Phew!' she exclaimed, laughing ruefully as she almost fell from the car, feeling sticky all over from the enervating heat.

Amélie merely shrugged, her eyes appraising on Eve's hot face. 'The sun does not bother me,' she replied coolly. 'You see, *ma chère*, I am used to it, having lived here all my life.'

Meaning I haven't, I suppose! Eve got the message loud and clear, although she bit back a sharp retort. In a way, Amélie was probably right, and it couldn't be a subject worth quarrelling over! And it was a bit late to begin doubting her wisdom in coming here with Amélie today. It might be better to try and suppress a too vivid imagination! Amélie would never dare harm her, Eve felt sure.

The car was parked and locked on a piece of dry ground before they set off along the side of a swamp. Amélie, Eve was forced to admit before they had gone very far, was a wonderful guide. She seemed to possess a boundless store of sharp energy and soon had found numerous nests. As it was spring the air was alive with the sound of birds, and soon the loneliness of the terrain wasn't so noticeable any more as Amélie named various species, pointing out the wonderful construction of some of the nests. One in particular, that of the whiskered tern which built a floating one of bulrushes and sedge stems, intrigued Eve a lot.

It was much later when Amélie discovered she had forgotten to bring the picnic basket, that they hadn't so much as a flask of fresh water, let alone tea! They had reached a point bordering the edge of the lake, or *étang*, as lakes were called here, when Amélie decided she could go no further without a drink.

'It is all my fault!' she wailed charmingly, when they returned to the car and found what had happened. '*Tiens*, and I am parched!' she exclaimed.

'Well, it won't have to matter.' Eve was feeling parched herself, but had no intention of complaining. Anyone could make such a mistake. 'It might be better,' she conjectured, 'to simply go home.' In fact she had a sudden, inexplicable longing to do so.

But Amélie wouldn't hear of it. 'It is scarcely four o'clock,' she cried. 'There is still so much I have to show you, especially when, as Raoul has told me, you are soon to be leaving us for London. You must wait here. I will return to the *mas* to collect our tea. On my own I will go much quicker and should be back within half an hour, no more.'

With a regrettable flicker of relief, Eve gazed after the departing car. Amélie just wouldn't take no for an answer, declaring adamantly that as the fault was entirely hers she couldn't object to the bother. Eve hadn't persisted, her desire to return to the ranch fading before an even stronger wish to remain where she was and brood. It was not the first time Amélie had related Raoul's remarks, yet always the hurt seemed fresh. Maybe Amélie did do it deliberately, with a touch of exaggeration, but somewhere, Eve frowned, there must be a glimmer of truth. Whatever, it might certainly be advisable to see what she could while she had the chance, and it was strangely soothing, in spite of her former apprehension, to sit here alone.

Eve settled beneath a rather ragged-looking white poplar, the nearest large tree she could find, and prepared to wait. Amélie had told her not to explore on her own, and for once Eve didn't feel like disobeying. The heat seemed to have made her quite tired and she yawned, content to watch a distant group of flamingoes taking off from the lake, the red feathers under their wings, which were hidden when folded, like a brilliant flash of flame against the sky.

Afterwards, Eve never could remember the exact moment she fell asleep, but she always remembered how stiffly uncomfortable she felt when she woke over two hours later. How apprehensive she was when she realised she was still alone, there being no sign of Amélie with the picnic basket. For a few moments she sat where she was, frowning, trying to ponder constructively on what might have happened. Was it possible that Amélie, driving as she did, had met with an accident? It was now—Eve glanced again at her slim wrist—after six o'clock, and Amélie had been gone since four. There could, of course, be other explanations, if one had time to think them out, but one or two things seemed very clear. If Amélie had had an accident then it was highly improbable she would be back, but unless she was unconscious she could surely have told someone about her? The men from the ranch would have been here very quickly. But, so far as she could see, there wasn't a soul in sight.

For another half hour Eve waited, before deciding she must walk. It seemed too obvious that Amélie, or help of any kind, wasn't coming, and it seemed senseless to stay here until dark. Wryly, as she rose to her feet, Eve glanced down at the place where she had been sitting. She didn't think she would ever forget these thirty minutes—the silver trees, the lake and flamingoes; the bare plain and, in the distance, a faint line of white horses grazing towards her. It helped, by concentrating on them, to overlook the peculiar trickle of fear which crept down her spine, making her tremble.

Briefly she hesitated, having little idea of her exact position or of the general direction she should take. The air was still warm, but her skin felt clammy and cold as she became slowly aware what it must be like to spend the night here in the open, alone. There was, she saw, with great relief, the marks of Amélie's car tyres, but though she followed these for what must have been the most part of a mile they eventually faded out as she reached drier ground.

Nevertheless, trying to use some common sense, Eve trudged on, keeping the sun determinedly on her right as she went along. The initial shock at being deserted in such a wilderness had faded yet taken its toll. Her hair was damp, clinging to her cheeks, and perspiration had soaked her thin shirt, which was now crumpled and dirty. Her jeans and shoes were soaked in mud from falling into a swamp, and wide-eyed she surveyed them, feeling only a half hysterical relief that Raoul DuBare, with his fastidious fault-finding, couldn't see her now.

It seemed to come to her only slowly that all about her was growing quieter. As night approached the birds ceased singing, there was only the rustle of wind in the tops of the pines. The treetops were glowing with the rays of the setting sun and the glinting light moved from leaf to leaf, dancing between the branches before subsiding into the olive-green canopy of shrubs and thick undergrowth. Then she was aware all around her of new noises and sounds, of shadows detaching themselves from the dark reed tunnels among the marshes and turning into hungry, searching creatures bent on foraging for food under the protection of the oncoming darkness. It was then, to her horror, that she heard what seemed to be a grunt, and remembering what Amélie had said about wild boars, she took to her heels and ran, spending what little breath she had left in one last depairing race to escape what she imagined could be a relentless pursuer.

Needless to say nothing did actually chase after her, but it was perhaps just as well that the noise had sent her off in another direction, as it was only after she had forced her way through a heavy clump of shrub that the *gardians* found her.

They assured her that they had never for a moment doubted they would, although relief mingled with disbelief on their faces as Eve burst into sight. Céleste did tell her later that they had all been terribly worried, especially as Raoul hadn't been there to direct them, and they had not immediately found her where Amélie had sworn she would be.

'The danger,' Céleste said, 'of being lost in the Delta comes not so much from being attacked by wild animals as from the possibility of falling into one of the numerous lakes or swamps.'

Most of the *gardians* had searched for her on horseback, but two of them came in trucks, and it was into one of these that the men gently put Eve to drive her home, trying, she could see, not to look too closely at her bedraggled appearance. Fortunately, apart from this, she seemed none the worse; at least she wasn't fainting all over the place, as she had thought she might when her control had seemed to be slipping—when, for one awful moment, she had decided no one would ever find her again. For the first time in her life she had felt numb with fear as she had visualised a devilish pursuer in the scrub. Death, she remembered thinking, could be relentless, but could surely never overtake her like this!

Her face felt sore where deep scratches had cut the white skin, and when she touched the red weals with exploratory fingers she winced, glad again that Raoul wasn't here to see her. He was in Paris, thank goodness. Yet contrarily her flicker of relief brought no real comfort. He would be back!

When she found her voice sufficiently to ask the men what exactly had happened to Amélie, they looked peculiarly evasive, muttering something about engine trouble, which to Eve's dazed mind sounded just about right. No reason for them to reply in such uncertain tones, or, when they concluded that she was too spent to hear, to whisper together so apprehensively about *le maître*. Nothing of what had happened was their fault—anyone's fault, really, so what had they to worry about? Hadn't they rescued her, and wasn't Raoul hundreds of miles away. And, before he came back, she might even be as far away from this terrible place herself.

It was Céleste who eventually told her exactly what had

happened. Amélie, it seemed, shortly after she had left Eve that afternoon, had developed a fault in her engine and had decided to make for Les Saintes Maries. The garage there, she had felt sure, would be able to sort out the trouble quicker than they could at the ranch. But it had been several hours before she had even got there, and a while longer before a mechanic diagnosed dirt in the petrol tank and pronounced that he could do little about it that night.

'So it was almost dark, you see, before Amélie rang here asking us to go and fetch you,' Céleste said anxiously. 'I think she blamed herself for not finding it possible to let us know sooner. I think she said it was a case of acting for the best and nothing turning out as she'd expected!'

And she could say that again! Eve thought wryly, as she surveyed her mutilated arms and face in the mirror next morning. Amélie hadn't, in fact, arrived back until after Eve the night before, and she had been full of commiseration, none of which, to Eve's weary ears at least, sounded particularly sincere. Amélie's story was too plausible. If there had been dirt in the engine, wouldn't it have troubled them on the way to the reserve earlier in the afternoon? It didn't seem possible—and certainly wouldn't be probable; she had deliberately put it there herself so that Eve might be forced to spend the night alone on the marshes, but Eve shivered, knowing suddenly beyond doubt, that what she suspected was true.

Yet why should Amélie Troyat do such a thing? Had she quite ruthlessly wanted to drive a girl she disliked out of her mind? Eve shuddered, remembering her own terror, wondering wildly if it could have happened. That Amélie should constructively plan such an occurrence surely indicated some degree of derangement. No wholly sane person would ever think of such a thing!

Agonisingly, all through the night, while her bruises and sore limbs refused to let her rest, Eve thought of it, and long before dawn pushed tentative fingers across her windowsill she knew what she must do. She might have misjudged Amélie, but she couldn't afford, for Michel's sake, to give her the benefit of this doubt. Raoul must not be allowed to marry Amélie, as he had indicated he might if Eve kept on refusing him. If Amélie really was unstable, then might it not be almost criminal to allow her any part in Michel's future, especially when the way to prevent this was clearly indicated?

As if to confirm her suspicions, Amélie came to her room first thing the next morning, suggesting lightly but firmly, 'Don't you think you would be wise to go home immediately, Eve? Your face is scratched, but not too badly, nothing to stop you travelling. I could quite easily accompany you as far as Paris today, which would certainly guarantee your escape from Raoul's anger when he returns.'

Her heart suddenly cold, Eve laid aside the small hand mirror she had been holding and stared at Amélie in confusion. So Amélie was determined to be rid of her after all—and today! She was certainly a woman of some decision, was Amélie! Dryly Eve swallowed, feeling a great necessity to gulp the tea Amélie had dropped sharply on her bedside table, but dared not. It could be poisoned! Half hysterically she giggled softly at her own humour.

Amélie, seeing only the hectic spots of colour on Eve's pale cheeks, sought deviously to press her point. 'You could never stand up to Raoul's anger, *ma chère*. His wealth makes him arrogant. You are too small and vulnerable.'

Eve blinked in some confusion, sobering right away before the flaring spark in Amélie's eye. 'I know he is impatient of accidents, *madame*, and I realise I have had several since I came here, but none of them, especially this last one, was my fault. Well, not exactly . . .'

As her voice trailed off Amélie countered sharply, 'But if you hadn't insisted on going to the game reserve——'

'But I didn't!' Eve's eyes widened with bewilderment. 'It was you who suggested it, you know that.'

'But no one else does, and who will believe you?' Amélie's laughter was spiteful. 'Raoul is too aware of my dislike for any part of the countryside, the reserve, with all those thousands of screaming, highly colourful birds, especially. And he knows better than most that I am not to be persuaded to do anything I would not enjoy.'

'He wouldn't believe you!'

'He very probably would.' Amélie's black eyes snapped. 'And then you would also be a liar, as well as a nuisance, *ma chère*.'

Eve felt stunned, also slightly sick with a great upsurge of foreboding. If she had been seeking for confirmation regarding the state of Amélie's mind, didn't she have it now? All the evidence she needed—if she only had to convince herself. Nothing else must be important, all her personal inclinations must be clamped down on. Carol, Dominique, her uncle and aunt would never forgive her if she let Michel down now.

For one distraught moment she closed her eyes against the inevitable. There was a chance, if a slim one, that such a decision might never have to be made, that Raoul might believe Amélie and consider this latest escapade of Eve's unforgivable and wash his hands of her. Involuntarily she flinched against the confusing pain of such a possibility, tremors which went shattering through her dismissing coherent thought. In such an event she could only make one last attempt to make alternative plans for Michel.

Amélie moved, sharply impatient, her eyes glacial on Eve's hesitant face. 'Well, *mademoiselle*,' she prompted, 'are you deaf as well as blind?'

'I'm sorry,' Eve whispered, her nausea strangely deepening before the insolence in Amélie's voice, 'I'm afraid I can't go home today, *madame*. Raoul might, as you say, very easily be furious, but whatever else I may be, I hope I am not a coward. I must stay and see him.'

CHAPTER NINE

Eve, understandably, was a little late in coming down for breakfast that morning and was surprised to find Céleste in the hall, already dressed to go out.

As she heard Eve on the stairs, Céleste glanced upwards with an unusual air of startled embarrassment colouring her smoothly made-up cheeks. 'Oh, hello, *ma chère*,' she said brightly, obviously pushing aside her confusion. 'Amélie tells me you are fully recovered, so you won't mind if I go with her to Marseille. We are to collect her car from the garage in Les Saintes Maries. She is waiting outside for me now, and asked me to hurry.'

'Yes—well, fine. Go ahead.' Eve's lips felt strangely stiff. It seemed an effort to speak carelessly, as though Céleste's desertion didn't matter. Somehow everything was an effort this morning in spite of the fact that she must be relatively unscathed from her ordeal. It brought some small relief, however, to know that Amélie was going, although Eve doubted it would be for long. In another way her going didn't seem to make sense—hadn't she threatened to tell Raoul the wrong story? It seemed unlikely that she had had second thoughts and changed her mind.

Céleste, gathering up her handbag, soon enlightened her. 'Raoul rang and Amélie answered, before I came down. She has explained about yesterday, but she didn't say what he said. He has a conference this morning, so will not be home before this evening or maybe tomorrow. But do not look so worried, *ma chère*, he can't be angry!'

But he was angry, furiously angry, and he arrived home in the middle of the afternoon, when Eve least expected him.

'Céleste told me you had a conference,' she gasped, as her

bedroom door was rudely thrust open and he strode in unannounced.

She was lying on her bed, fully clothed in one of the shapeless cotton frocks from her wardrobe, to which, after Raoul's dry criticism, she had taken an inexplicable dislike, only wearing it now because it was cool against her burning skin. Fervently she wished he hadn't found her like this, but the hot sunshine outside had made the scratches on her face sting, forcing her indoors, and somehow it had seemed sensible to curl up on her bed. How she regretted this now! Raoul's sudden appearance put her in a fine fret and she clenched her hands hard to stop them trembling.

'What happened to your conference?' she tried again, as he made no reply to her first query.

'*Mon dieu!*' It appeared to have taken him several seconds to find his voice, and he swore roundly, not beneath his breath, as his eyes blazed over her torn face, her sore young body huddled helplessly against the pillows. He rapped out an oath which was only surpassed by his glowering expression. 'You talk of conferences, *mademoiselle*, but leave me with no peace of mind to concentrate. The moment my back is turned you seem all set to commit suicide, and I am forced to rush home to survey the damage!' Ruthlessly he sank down beside her on the bed, his hand going out to sweep the tumbled gold curls from her face. '*Mon dieu!*' he repeated, 'if you had set out deliberately to ruin your beautiful skin you could not have done better!'

'It was scarcely my fault, *monsieur*.' His close proximity made her voice weak and she lay very still, aware of an urgent need to placate him before he added to the damage she had already sustained.

Coldly he continued to regard her. 'Did I not promise to take you to the reserve myself? As a member, I have access to every part of it. But no, you must assert your insane independence by going yourself, by begging Amélie to take you. My patience,' his jaw clamped, 'is at an end! I refuse to spend my entire future quoting parrot-like, "you might have been killed"! From this minute onwards, *ma cherie*, you will not so much as move until you have my absolute permission!'

'But it wasn't like that...' Near breaking point, Eve gazed at him, Amélie's words returning triumphantly to haunt her—'he will only think you are a liar'. Could she, risk this—would it not perhaps be better to let things slide? After all, no crime was involved, and matters might merely be made worse. Yet somehow there was in Eve the most fervent compulsion to protest, even though Raoul's darkness, his cold purpose was most intimidating, doing nothing to encourage a plea for understanding.

'You tell me how it was like?' he ground out sarcastically as she paused. 'Then you will no doubt feel better, which is more than I can ever hope to do.'

His ambiguity was beyond her. It was his tone of voice that prompted her to continue recklessly, 'To go to the reserve wasn't my idea. You might recall saying, before you left yesterday, that I needed fresh air, and after lunch, Amélie suggested we went there.'

'Eve!' His green eyes darkened coldly to jet, and she knew immediately she had made a mistake. On his face was no sign of the trust she had hoped for, only suspicion, an almost tangible longing to shake her. 'I wish,' he was suddenly taut, 'you could lose this rather stupid habit of lying to me. Amélie would never dream of going near the reserve. It is too tied up with memories of her husband. She dislikes it intensely.'

'Then there is nothing more to be said, *monsieur*,' Eve's face went white, the shock of his incredulity worse to bear than any physical pain she was suffering. 'You must surely be congratulating yourself that you discovered my true character in time.'

'Before I married you, you mean?' His eyes were like diamond slits in the hardness of his face.

'Exactly.' Gloriously defiant, Eve annihilated all her former resolutions. Never, never could she marry such an arrogant man!

His voice was smoothly suave. 'But you mustn't let it bother you, *mon amie*. I intend to iron all such deception from you, if necessary with a heavy hand. You are young enough to learn. *Mon dieu*, you won't know yourself when I am finished!'

She flung at him her furious retort, 'I like myself as I am, *monsieur*!'

'*Monsieur*,' he mocked cruelly, his eyes contemptuous of her spirited protest, before his expression changed abruptly, and it seemed in spite of himself, as again his frowning glance rested on the livid marks on her otherwise smooth white throat. 'I must have a look at those scratches,' he went on, somewhat curtly, 'so you can stop acting like an outraged child and oblige me by being still for a moment. Marie informs me that you refused to allow her to send for the doctor!'

'Well, it wasn't necessary . . .'

His mouth thinned. 'But I, *mademoiselle*, will arrange that he shall come immediately, should I feel it necessary.'

Eve squirmed sullenly, trying not to flinch as he began to examine her face very thoroughly, her hand clenched tight when once he probed too closely. Yet his fingers were infinitely gentle, his movements deft, and she could find no real cause for complaint. It was when he saw the deeper weals on her shoulders that his fingers stiffened as though he would have liked to hit her. 'And you got up, this morning,' he rasped, 'and went down to breakfast, telling everyone you were well!'

'I suppose Amélie assured you she would not have left if she had thought otherwise?' Eve choked, almost breathless with an unhappiness she didn't understand and hating his seeming indifference.

'One more word,' he ground out, the hardness of his

green glance cold on her lacerated skin, 'and I will add to your pain where it hurts most. Naturally neither Amélie or Céleste would have left if they had known. Now if you will make some endeavour to relax I will dress these wounds properly, before ringing the good doctor.'

'I wish you wouldn't, Raoul,' she begged, her eyes fixed pleadingly on his, not really surprised when he refused.

'There may be some infection, *ma chère*, as you must with your training know. Only a doctor can deal with that!'

It seemed hours later, but was actually just after eight o'clock, when Eve, bathed and dressed, joined Raoul for dinner in the cool dimness of the dining-room. The doctor had arrived and given her an injection, but declared himself unable to improve on Raoul's initial treatment. He had examined her so thoroughly that she suspected Raoul's implicit instructions, then, with Marie looking on, had informed her that with a little care she should soon heal, that she was indeed a very fortunate young lady.

If she sensed undertones of another meaning apart from her health, the doctor's suave countenance gave no clues. She had no clear idea what he was on about until she took coffee with Raoul in his study later in the evening. When he told her, without a fraction of hesitation, they were to be married in a few days' time.

'I have been making all the necessary arrangements in Paris,' he said coolly, apparently oblivious of Eve's speechless stare. 'We will be married there but return here immediately, as Nadine and Céleste will leave the same day on a six months' tour of the States. Afterwards, *ma chère*, we will be away on our own vacation, a belated honeymoon, if you like.'

Eve's eyes widened and she felt dizzy and grasped the cup she was holding until her knuckles shone white. He had been extremely considerate over dinner and she had come down not knowing quite what to expect, the recollection of his total disbelief in her integrity colouring her imagination as a forerunner of escalating disaster. It was no comfort to learn that her instincts had not been wrong. 'You go about things in a very high-handed manner,' she whispered hoarsely.

Firmly he eased the fragile cup from her taut fingers, his dark eyes narrowed on her shocked face. 'Otherwise,' he emphasised, 'we should never get anywhere. We both know what we must do for Michel and an impossible situation is fast developing, one which I hope to deal with very quickly once we are married. There comes a time when it is necessary to take action, Eve.'

He talked in riddles, as usual, and her mind was too numbed to sort it out. Hopelessly, in spite of all her former resolutions, she knew what she must do, but what about him? Uncertainty flickered, distress turning her pupils to an almost intense blue. 'You are willing,' she asked nervously, 'to sacrifice all hope of marrying someone you love?'

He said, very crisply, his eyes glinting with a kind of devilment, 'Don't you visualise any romance between us?'

'I don't think so,' her heavy lashes swept her cheeks as she faltered, not daring to let him so much as glimpse at her despair. 'You would not find me very exciting, *monsieur*.'

His mouth quirked. 'You might surprise me.'

The need to be completely honest drove her beyond her normal discretion. 'I don't think I have a passionate nature . . .'

'You have some evidence of this?' There was still the touch of amusement, the indication that he refused to take this matter seriously.

Unhappily Eve was beginning to wish she had never said anything, but once started, what else could she do but go on? 'I've never had a serious affair, *monsieur*, and I have had the opportunity, but you see I have never felt particularly amorous.'

'And what if I told you I am willing to take a chance?'

'I wouldn't wish you to feel cheated.'

This time his voice came very smoothly. 'I do not anticipate such an event.'

Immediately she went taut, something moving convulsively in the pit of her stomach. She felt all sorts of things about him instinctively, but this was one thing—the ability to find the right words to express such feelings, quite another. 'What you are saying, *monsieur*, seems to suggest that you imagine a normal marriage. Or perhaps that you expect to seek some sort of distraction elsewhere?'

His eyes scorched her face with their cynical amusement, and he appeared in no way impressed by her obviously painful endeavours to have everything straightened out between them. His light laughter flicked her lazily as he drawled, 'And why should I go to the trouble and the often considerable expense of keeping another woman when I will have a young and beautiful wife, who is probably only lacking a little careful tuition?'

His teasing was the last straw. Her face scarlet with mortification, she cried, 'You must give me time!' In a breathing space anything could happen, a reprieve had been won in less.

His eyes narrowed comprehendingly, but he merely said, 'Just so long as you don't ask for a written guarantee, *ma chère*. You British are very keen on your guarantees.'

'But you are a man of your word?' Feebly she clutched at anything.

'Usually, but do not try me too far, *petite*. I might also be something rather beyond your experience.'

What did he mean? He was French, of course, which did not necessarily mean he disliked all English girls, although he had disapproved of Carol. 'You didn't like my cousin did you, *monsieur*?'

His lips thinned impatiently, although he replied evenly enough. 'I can't see how that odd little question has any bearing on the present situation, Eve, and I don't think it would profit either of us to discuss either Carol or my brother. I will see to it that their child is well looked after, but they can't, unfortunately, have any part in his future.'

Unhappily Eve stared away from him. So he intended marrying her with the mystery of Carol and Dominique like a blank wall between them? Which only implied that he didn't altogether trust her? And, come to that, in other ways perhaps the mistrust was mutual. Would he really find it possible to give up all his girl-friends—especially Amélie? Eve found herself doubting it.

Suddenly, as her eyes returned widely to his, he pulled her decisively to her feet. 'Come, *ma chère*,' he ordered lightly, 'you've had enough drama in the last few days without adding to it. I'll see you to your room, otherwise I fear you might collapse on the way up—you have an air of fine exhaustion.'

Somehow she found it impossible to argue, to find so much as a whisper of protest as, with his hand protectively beneath her arm, Raoul halted outside her bedroom door.

'Now,' he said, his mockery cancelling the solicitude of a moment ago, 'say goodnight like a good girl. There is always tomorrow.'

Without giving her a chance to protest, he bent his dark head and kissed her, his lips crushing hers hard. It was only briefly, but the touch of that ruthless mouth was enough to send a blaze of fire shooting through her, bringing chaos to her emotions.

'Goodnight, *chérie*,' she heard his voice coolly following her, as, anything but coolly, she wrenched herself free and fled into her room.

They were married, as Raoul had promised, five days later, the ceremony brief, in the same church where he told her his parents had been married almost forty years ago. It was all very quiet, with only Céleste and Nadine and an old friend of Raoul's, a man of about the same age, who seemed quite taken with Eve and embarrassed her by declaring emphatically to Raoul that he was marrying a beautiful *jeune fille*. She wasn't surprised to learn later that he was a member of the old French nobility—such sophistication and elegance would have been impossible to place elsewhere.

The day before the wedding she had travelled to Paris with Raoul and Céleste and the two girls had stayed overnight with Nadine. Eve was still not quite sure exactly how Céleste had taken the news of the impending marriage, but Raoul had given her little opportunity to air any definite views, if indeed she had any. In Raoul's presence she had hinted rather sharply to Eve that there had been no necessity to carry their little charade so far. And to Raoul she had protested that Amélie would be heartbroken. But before she had got any further Raoul had whipped her curtly into his study, to deliver, Eve had little doubt, a lecture. While she could sympathise with Céleste's bewilderment she had felt oddly grateful for the ensuing silence when Céleste, obviously enthralled with the prospect of America, had held her peace.

Only once, that Eve knew of, did she relate to the subject again. 'I never thought,' Eve heard her say smugly to Raoul before they went in to the reception, 'that when I sent for Eve to come to the Camargue it would turn out like this!'

But there had been no time for Raoul to reply, or to even suppose he had heard properly, and, in the next champagne-drinking, congratulation-filled hours, no opportunity for him to question Céleste, if he had been inclined. Céleste's mood veered so changeably that Eve saw, not for the first time, she would always need a steadying influence in her life, and, fond as she was of her, Eve felt strangely thankful she would be away for six months.

It seemed inconsistent with her relief that the ceremony was over to feel a curious reluctance when she and Raoul left Paris to return home later in the afternoon. She would have liked to have lingered, but Raoul wished only to get back.

As he heard her low sigh, his lips moved in a slight smile.

'Paris is really for lovers,' he said, clearly reading her thoughts, 'to be enjoyed to the full. But,' he added, enigmatically, 'I promise you will see it another day.'

Eve bit her lip, looking down at her lap, a demure and attractive figure in her cool silk dress. It was a dress which had cost more than she had dared think about, and, though it had been purchased in a hurry the previous morning along with several others, fitted her beautifully. She tried, but failed dismally, to keep her thoughts away from the fashionable boutique she had been taken to. 'The leading couturière, the most expensive in the city!' Céleste had whispered, proceeding to reel off the names of some of its famous clientele before Raoul had growled at her to shut up.

It would have been sensible to have shown how humiliated she had felt, having scarcely enough money to pay for the shoes she had been married in, yet for a little while she had found it possible to be completely captivated by the ankle-length, frothy white dress which Raoul insisted she wore in church. There was also a collection of equally suitable gowns which had been sent this morning for her to take home.

And that hadn't been all. In the late afternoon there had been a lengthy visit to the luxurious salon of a famous beauty house where she had been gone over, it seemed, from head to toe, everything possible being done to turn her from a passably pretty girl into a raving beauty. Certainly Eve had found it rather difficult to recognise herself afterwards—all the gleaming, satiny skin, the enchantingly pure curve of a sensuous mouth, a fluffy fall of ashen hair, fingers so delicately tinted as to give every appearance of not having done so much as a day's work in their life. Yet every bit of her ironic self criticism had been forgotten before the glittering appreciation in Raoul's eyes as she had walked towards him up the aisle.

'You look wonderful, *chérie*,' she had thought he had said, but wasn't sure she had heard him correctly above the frantic beating of her own heart. 'Beautiful . . .'

It was late when they arrived back at the ranch and there was no one about. Even the nursery, which was on the other side of the huge house, was quiet. Tactfully, Marie had laid out a cold meal in the dining room, and, after wishing them every joy, she discreetly withdrew, but not without a glance of complete approval at Eve's flushed, embarrassed face.

'She only presumes you are covered with a very proper confusion,' Raoul teased softly, as he removed her coat. 'But that is nothing to what you might expect tomorrow,' he smiled. 'It is not every day that *le maître* is married. The *gardians* will have a feast and no doubt celebrate accordingly. I might even get a little drunk myself, *ma chère*, if you continue to look at me as you do now.'

Hastily Eve removed her wide-eyed gaze from his grave face, excusing herself quickly to go and wash her hands. A few days ago it had all seemed comparatively easy, but now she was beginning to realise that her difficulties might only just be starting. Raoul had hinted that there would be celebrations. Did he forget they had married simply for the sake of the child? She would liked to have reasserted this point, but somehow she dared not, something intangible in the man himself stopping her. It almost seemed beyond her to carry on even a normal conversation.

Swiftly she ran upstairs. The journey had been hot and tedious, and she felt a sudden longing to freshen up completely, to find an old pair of more comfortable shoes for her aching feet. To her utter surprise, when she pushed open the door to her room it was empty. The furniture had not been removed, of course, but the bed was stripped and bare and the wardrobe stood open—bereft of all clothes.

As she stared apprehensively, her heart thudding uncertainly, she heard Raoul's footsteps coming up behind her. 'You are naturally with me now, *ma chère*,' he said coolly, his hands forcibly on her shoulders as he paused with her, surveying the room.

If Eve felt in his fingers some urgency transmitting itself

into her soft flesh she ignored it, holding herself rigid, determined to resist the wild impulse to turn and fling herself wholly into his arms. Also to be curbed was the very real possibility of traitorous senses turning all this into some old-fashioned melodrama. A little common sense was all that might be required—to remain sane.

'I would rather have stayed here, at least for a little while longer.' She tried to speak evenly, but her words didn't come out that way.

If he was aware of her agitation he took no notice. His hands merely tightened. 'Perhaps you would, Eve, but I do not wish that we should become the objects of amused speculation, as would surely happen if you remained here.'

'But you promised!' In spite of her resolve to be sensible her voice rose, as she wrenched furiously round to face him.

His eyes narrowed darkly at her obvious temper. 'I made no promises about anything,' he said quietly, 'least of all about this.'

'Just because we never had time to get around to it, but I should have thought it was understood!' she flashed bitterly. 'Anyway,' she stepped hastily backwards, 'whether you approve or not I refuse to move! And, as I feel very tired, I don't think I'll come down again, so I'll say goodnight!'

It was a mistake to get hysterical, to goad him. Immediately she spoke she knew that, but she wasn't in any way prepared for his reactions. Like steel bands his arms went around her, scooping her up, scattering the handbag she was carrying and its contents across the floor as he turned with brute force, crushing her to him as he slammed the door and strode relentlessly along the wide corridor outside.

Eve became aware that she was screaming, half choking against his hard chest, and the more noise she made the more livid he became, clasping her so tightly it hurt. Then, when she seemed almost to have lost all breath, she felt herself released, flung down, or rather hurled, on to something soft—a bed.

'Goodnight, *madame*!' His voice, like a hard living flame, seemed to scorch her. 'I no more wish for an unwilling bride than you obviously wish to be one. I can assure you you will not be disturbed here!'

Eve gasped, but before she could speak, if she could have found the words to do so, he had turned and was gone, the door rocking on its hinges emphatically behind him.

Next morning she wasn't sure it hadn't been all a nightmare, but during her first awakening moments when she saw she was completely alone, she slowly realised it had actually happened, her memory wasn't just playing her tricks. Raoul had been completely infuriated, and now must be wholly antagonised, something she had never honestly intended should occur, and even now could not clearly understand how it had come about.

Unhappily her glance travelled around the room she now occupied. She must be in Raoul's private suite on the west side of the house, where she had never been before. Her bathroom door stood open, but there was another door, obviously a communicating one which she hadn't dared try the previous night. In case, she recalled thinking wildly, he was on the other side!

No doubt, she hazarded, her glance lingering, that would be his bedroom. Or maybe it was just a dressing-room and she was actually in the bed Raoul usually used. It was large enough and on the dressing-table was laid out what appeared to be a masculine set of brushes. A feeling of something very like shame ran through her, along with a definite quiver of misery as she considered, in retrospect, her own questionable behaviour. There could have been no real need to act as she had done. When they had first arrived home Raoul had not seemed as if he was preparing to be unreasonable. Now she had alienated him completely, he would probably not even be willing to be remotely friendly. And could she blame him? She might justifiably resent his mistrust of her, but had she not exaggerated her own attraction in imagining he wanted her as a man would normally want his wife?

Confused, and not a little embarrassed by her own racing thoughts, Eve scrambled out of bed, and after having a quick shower ran downstairs, Marie, for some reason, had not brought coffee, and Eve suddenly longed for some. Her suitcases had been left inside her bedroom door, although she had no idea how they had got there. Someone must have entered the room silently when she had fallen into an exhausted sleep just before dawn. From an array of new, expensive dresses Eve chose a soft, round-necked cotton, which was cool and hid the now almost faded evidence of her adventure in the nature reserve.

At first she did not look for Raoul, instead she sought Marie in the kitchen.

'But it is in the dining room, *madame*.' Wryly Eve noticed the new, formal address, but let it go.

'I . . .' she stammered, suddenly aware of Marie's openly curious stare, 'I—I missed my early morning cup and didn't want to go straight in for breakfast.'

'*Le maître* said neither of you might want any this morning,' Marie said bluntly, reaching consideringly for the coffee pot, her meaning so clear that Eve felt herself go hot all over.

How dared Raoul give such an order! How dared he, she kept repeating, silently furious as Marie's eyes went slowly over her. Swiftly she assured the woman she had changed her mind about the coffee and ran out into the gardens.

If Raoul had accused her of contriving to give the servants food for thought, it was apparent that he didn't think twice about committing the same crime himself. During that first day and the next she scarcely saw him except at mealtimes, when the conversation on both sides could only be described as cool, studiously polite. Occasionally he was attentive enough, to allay, she supposed, speculation. The *gardians* had had their day of celebration which Eve concluded, unbearably, neither she nor Raoul had enjoyed very much. She had scarcely drunk anything herself and Raoul had remained stone cold sober.

It was this prevailing coldness that frightened Eve most, his ability to remain completely detached while she worked herself into a fine if incomprehensible fret of unhappiness. Her own private hell which grew almost past bearing. She lost a little weight, her inner turmoil reflected in a loss of appetite and a growing conviction that Raoul was beginning to mean more than she had ever thought possible.

It was this knowledge which she refused to face that prompted her to seek the isolation of the vast steppes on the third afternoon after their return from Paris. She had spent most of the day with Michel, already loving the boy and confident she had his affection in return. Eve hadn't been altogether surprised that Michel's grandparents approved of her marrying Raoul, because, she suspected, they would imagine this ensured Michel's future. But they had also, she knew, been overjoyed when Raoul had asked them to visit whenever they liked. It would seem that everything could end happily in this direction, if nothing else.

Raoul had been gone since lunch—something to do, he had explained briefly, with the next day's festivities in Les Saintes Maries de la Mer. He had not asked Eve to accompany him, and suddenly, after tea, she could bear the confines of the house no longer on her own. She would go riding; it seemed an age since she had been out on the little horse she usually rode. There was an eagerness inside her to have the wind wild on her face, through her hair, anything which might remove the increasing lethargy of the last few days.

Even to think of it made her feel better and she ran quickly upstairs. She would have to change into something suitable—the dress she was wearing certainly wouldn't do, but it wasn't until she reached her old room that she remembered her old clothes had disappeared. When she had mentioned this before to Raoul he had merely said he had instructed Marie to burn them, which had annoyed Eve so much she had been unable to make any comment, but surely he must have realised she would need something to ride in? Frowning, she stood before the empty wardrobe wondering what to do. There was just a chance Marie might not yet have got around to disposing of them, especially her jeans.

In the kitchen Marie glanced at her dubiously. 'They are still in the old laundry, *madame*. I'm afraid I forgot all about them.'

Or more likely, Eve thought, Marie had intended giving them to some of her numerous relations, as there was nothing actually wrong with the clothes, except their cut, and the French were extremely thrifty. She felt Marie's eyes on her as she triumphantly rescued her jeans.

'Gracious,' she exclaimed disapprovingly, 'you are going to look shabby, *ma chère*, after the smart clothes you've been wearing!'

Eve ignored this, simply grinned like a young child as she clasped her trousers happily to her and, after thanking Marie, flew back upstairs. That had been easy! Off came the new expensive dress which made her look so appropriately elegant. With careless hands she let it drop to the floor before donning the somewhat faded, definitely untidy-looking short-sleeved shirt and slacks. They were comfortable and familiar and in them she felt free, curiously untrammelled by the tenacious threads of a marriage which wasn't really a marriage at all. Now she felt almost herself again, a carefree young girl belonging to no one. Outside she could hear the shrill, exultant cries of the birds, and in her heart was a sudden, exhilarating excitement, an echoing response to their free, wild song. The evening stretched before her, enticing her out to seek the solace, the soothing atmosphere of those lonely places for which the Camargue was famous. With any luck she should be back before Raoul.

Almost dancing she whipped around, to find to her dismay that he stood in the doorway, the very man she had hoped to avoid, staring at her. Her eyes widened darkly as a visible quiver went through her. How long had he been standing there?

She had heard nothing of him coming in—hadn't expected he would be home. Hadn't he told her he would probably be quite late, after dinner? He must have been in the bathroom which she knew he made use of at the other end of the corridor as he wore only a white towelling robe belted loosely around him, and his hair was still damp from the shower. He must have caught sight of her as he had been returning to his room, and Eve's nerves jerked painfully with a brilliant terror.

Trying desperately to beat down such frantic feelings of despair, her lips moved in a travesty of a casual smile. Did he have to look so utterly furious? Her heart, which only a few moments ago had been sailing gaily among the white clouds she had glimpsed from the window, dropped somewhere in the region of the boots she had not yet had time to put on. She had known herself to be afraid of him, but not how much!

It was plain to see he was mad about something, his green eyes glittered like daggers. 'Where were you going,' his voice cracked like a whip, 'dressed like that?'

So that was it! Helplessly, scarcely realising what she was doing, Eve blinked down at her crumpled jeans. 'I . . .' she had to swallow twice, 'I was simply going for a ride.'

'I refuse to allow you!'

'Oh, but . . .' Instinct warned her it would be wiser to offer some sort of explanation, to beg him to understand, but an inherent fear of rejection held her back. How could she hope to appeal to his better nature when he obviously didn't have one? Yet in spite of a consuming indignation, she had the grace to feel slightly ashamed when her evasive glance fell to the carelessly discarded dress and slip on the floor.

He stepped over the threshold, the first time he had ever

entered her room since that first disastrous night when he had flung her with such supreme indifference on to the bed. 'You are not,' he repeated tersely, a clear-cut determination in his mouth and chin, 'going anywhere in those clothes!'

'But,' her voice worked at last, and her eyes, intensely blue, clung to his face, 'I was only going riding, *monsieur*.'

'*Monsieur!*' he muttered some violent exclamation, his face black. 'After three days of marriage you can still call me that?'

She felt a little shiver of fear. She had known it was a mistake, but from habit it had just slipped out. 'It's nothing,' she muttered sullenly, 'to make a fuss about, but if you must have an apology, then I'm sorry!'

Such a reluctant expression of penitence was ignored. 'I will give you two seconds,' he said, the undertones of violence still in his voice, 'to get out of those unspeakable clothes, or I will remove them myself. It shouldn't be too difficult!'

CHAPTER TEN

STUNG by momentary shock, Eve flinched, her dazed glance flickering uncertainly before returning to his face, seeing the strength and purpose bred into it. Once he had spoken, he wasn't a man easily swayed from his word, but he mustn't be allowed to think she was so easily intimidated. 'You wouldn't dare!' she whispered emphatically. Too wholly on the defensive to be completely aware of the danger, she backed away from him, but he only advanced nearer, further into the room. Totally isolated as they were at this end of the great house, there was only silence as they stared at each other, tension beating, with almost tangible force, between them.

Desperately, as a panic she couldn't pinpoint rose within her, Eve glanced swiftly over her shoulder, measuring the distance to the bathroom door. Could she make it? She did manage a yard or two before he caught her—and then with an exclamation that scorched her already burning ears! Ruthlessly, as the moaning sound of the mistral rose outside, and clouds darkened stormily the evening sun, he dragged her to him, his hold inflexible as he gripped the top of her shirt and ripped, doing the same to her jeans. Upside down she seemed to go, the fury in his hands lending them strength, along with a surprising deftness, as he removed the offending garments and flung them remorselessly across the floor.

'Why, you beast!' Half sobbing in her fury, she tried to turn in his grasp to strike him. 'I hate you, I hate you!' she cried.

He pinned her pale, slender hands with one of his, rendering them ineffectual as his glance slid devastatingly over her.

'And so, *ma petite rebelle*, it will not matter how I treat you, you cannot dislike me more. But, *mon dieu*, I will only put up with so much!'

The heat of his anger burned into her, and before she could stop him he turned her to him, wholly into his arms, his eyes blazing down at her while the leashed look on his face stilled her to sheer breathlessness and fear fluttered like a wild thing through her breast.

Her breath came in a short, distressed little gasp. 'You're hurting me!' She pushed back against him, tears glinting with temper on her dilated pupils. 'You're a brute!' she cried, unable to keep the tremors from her voice as his hand moved over her. He was formidable, utterly ruthless, someone she scarcely knew.

'*Insolente!* You are greatly in need of a lesson, *madame*. It is time you learnt you can't have everything your own way!' Ruthlessly he crushed her to him, his hand beneath her chin, exploring the soft hollows of her throat as he forced her mouth up to meet his, the fierceness of his assault parting her bruised lips, striking a living flame right through her.

In one last sane instant Eve tried to resist, to fight free of the burning excitement which the hardness of his lips aroused within her. But Raoul refused to relent. He was all force and passion, stilling her feeble protests until, lost in a labyrinth of emotion, she ceased to struggle. Under his touch her shrinking disappeared, and there was only the feverish insistence of her blood pounding in her ears.

'I'll never let you go ...' His mouth lifted fractionally, his voice dark as his lips came down again, this time their pressure easing slightly as his hands probed the bareness of her skin through the ragged remains of her shirt. Eve moaned, turning in his arms, closer. Her heart was beating too fast, sensation hitting her in great waves, carrying her along on a tide of incomprehensible desire. Everything about her seemed to fall away, all her surroundings, even her own being whirling like a bursting dam about her ears as he drew from her slender body an ever increasing response.

'Raoul . . .' She wasn't wholly aware that she was sobbing his name, her lips moving numbly under his as she felt herself spinning out of control, her senses merely a roaring void in her ears. Her groping fingers touched the hard, smooth texture of his cheek, going slowly around his neck as she clung to him, her body going softly boneless against his.

'Raoul . . .' Tremors were attacking her limbs. Somewhere she was floating and he was lifting her, carrying her, but she had no knowledge of where he was going.

'Be still,' she heard his voice, thickly impatient. 'I don't wish to hurt you more than I must . . .'

'Raoul—please . . .' Was that her own voice trembling wildly before the passion in his?

'We are married, *mignonne*.' The pressure of his mouth and hands deepened, and was the last thing she seemed to hear, other than her own cry a little later before everything faded to unconsciousness.

The next day she went with Raoul to the festival in Les Saintes Maries de la Mer. She hadn't really wanted to go, but he had insisted, and it seemed she had no will left in her now to defy him. All morning Raoul and his men had been cutting bulls from the herds. These would be taken by lorry to the bull ring but brought back again afterwards and released to the herds. Bull breeding in the Camargue was directed at producing good *cocardiers*, bulls for the sport known in that area as the *course libre*, and animals bred for this could prove quite profitable for their owners.

The town itself was full of gipsies from all over Europe who gathered there each year on the twenty-fourth of May to attend Masses. Added to this, or mixed rather incongruously in with it, Eve thought, were the stirring songs, the celebrations in the streets, the bullfights where the ensuing dust seemed to mingle with the heavy scent of incense from the high altar. There was much to stare at, much to hold the attention of even the most jaded palate, but in spite of attempting determinedly to enjoy herself she was far from succeeding. To keep her mind wholly on the vivid entertainment all about her seemed impossible. She could only think of Raoul DuBare and his lovemaking, which in his case had nothing to do with love at all. Her own headlong response was something she tried in vain to forget. The night had been an experience she must somehow contrive to put from her.

The noise and gaiety that filled the little town seemed to be at an ever-increasing momentum. As she wandered through the crowds Raoul was never far from her side, remote yet curiously watchful, as if fully aware of her continuing lassitude and always ready when she occasionally stepped heedlessly into danger. It was late afternoon when the paleness of her face obviously prompted him to suggest they should seek some light refreshment, then return home. He would take her to a hotel.

'Your old friend Mrs Wood's establishment will do very well,' he said, 'and it will be quiet as it is out of town.'

Eve glanced at him woodenly, having no great desire to go there. 'It doesn't matter,' she hedged. 'I'd rather not, if you don't mind.'

'Oh, but I do, *ma chère*,' he replied thinly. 'If you must insist on wearing the air of a martyr then I must do something to cheer you up.'

Unhappily Eve refused to let him see how much his words hurt her. How could she ever have been crazy enough to imagine he might ever grow even remotely fond of a wife he had only chosen for convenience! He would look after her as he would any other investment, as part of his property, that was all. Towards her was always courteous, but suddenly this was far from enough. She wanted more.

Feeling it not worthwhile to protest further, she sat passively beside him as he drove swiftly to the hotel. Once there she felt relieved to see it was quiet, most of the guests still being in the town and not yet back to dress for dinner. Raoul ordered tea, a request, Eve mused, which wouldn't be too popular in the kitchens where, at this hour, they were no doubt preparing a celebration evening meal. Studiously, as they sat down, she kept her eyes averted, not needing to look at him to be aware of his faintly arrogant air of distinction, his undeniable good looks. How had she ever come to love a man like this? And love him she did—if it was something in the nature of an unwelcome shock to face the revelations of one's own heart! Previously her dislike had seemed to act as a sort of invisible reflector against the penetrating impact of his personality, but now, realising how she really felt appeared to remove all her defence mechanism and her subsequent vulnerability could only lead to further unhappiness, she was convinced.

Eve sat very still, her head bent slightly, allowing her fair, soft hair to fall over her cheek, hoping to hide her young despair. 'You may pour,' Raoul suggested when their tray arrived, and her hand went automatically out to grasp the teapot, shivering to hear him add, 'You've had very little all day, *ma chère*, and last night you did miss your dinner.'

Did he have to remind her? She had a feeling he did it deliberately, and it wasn't entirely one missed meal he was thinking of. 'I don't happen to be very hungry,' she replied as evenly as she could.

His glance, wholly encompassing, was full of restrained irritation, as though her silent distress was beyond him. 'Don't worry,' he said with seemingly cool indifference, 'your appetite is sure to return.'

Defensively she lifted her heavy lashes to glance at him mutinously, not caring for his sarcasm. 'It wasn't my fault——' she began, only to be cut off abruptly as none other than Mrs Wood bore down on them. Eve's breath caught uneasily. She had seen nothing of Mrs Wood since she had worked at the hotel, but had always felt guilty about leaving as she had, in such haste.

But Mrs Wood was obviously in the best of tempers, the presence of her former nursemaid, magically transmitted to the extremely enviable position of Madame DuBare, not affecting her adversely at all. Not on the face of it! 'Ah, *m'sieur, madame,*' she cried gaily, in the nature of a fully air-borne balloon, 'but how nice to see you!' Beaming, she wished them every happiness, expressing every hope of see-ing more of them in the future. 'And I also hope,' she appealed, smiling at Eve coyly, 'you can persuade your husband to open his riding stables again, dear. Nowadays I go elsewhere, but I miss the Manade DuBare very much.'

Eve glanced at Raoul uncertainly, seeing that he merely shrugged. Vaguely she remembered hearing something about this from Céleste, but couldn't recall anything de-finitely, and it didn't appear that Raoul was interested.

As if sensing this, Mrs Wood rushed on, 'This wasn't why I approached you today, *m'sieur.* It was actually about Madame Troyat.' As Raoul's eyebrows rose slightly, and Eve's heart jerked painfully, she continued, 'About two weeks ago she came in at this time and stayed on to dinner, and, I'm afraid, left her cigarette lighter. It is here,' she drew it out of her pocket, 'and it appears to be a good one. See, it has her initials. Well, the next morning, when I rang your house, I was told that she and your sister had already left for Marseille, and the next thing I knew your household was in Paris for your marriage, so I decided to leave it. I thought perhaps Madame Troyat might return to collect it herself . . .'

Mrs Wood talked for a few more minutes after passing to Raoul the elegant, gold-coloured lighter, then left them with a bright farewell and another fervently expressed wish about the riding stables. Dully Eve looked at the gleam of gold metal turning idly in Raoul's hands. It would merely serve to remind him of a woman he might have married, someone better able to match his demands than she. Before she could stop herself she said, 'You were very fond of Amélie . . .?'

'Fond!' The exclamation in his voice suggested she had understated, but curiously he said no more, just continued to frown contemplatively at the lighter.

Suddenly she didn't want to think any more about Amélie. 'This riding school?' she queried.

'It wasn't my idea,' he replied swiftly, obviously not concentrating on what she was saying, 'It was one of my brother's. It can be quite a profitable sideline with summer tourists, but I'm afraid I'm just not interested.'

'No, of course not.' Why were they conversing politely, like a couple of strangers? She took too quickly a gulp of hot tea, almost scalding herself.

'If you will excuse me, *ma chère*, I will be back in a moment.' Rising abruptly, his own tea apparently forgotten, Raoul left her without waiting for a reply.

All the way back to the manade Raoul was preoccupied, not talking very much, and Eve decided, the knowledge haunting her, that he was still thinking of Amélie. Even so, she was quite unprepared when, on arriving home, he said quietly, 'I have to go out again, *ma chère*.'

'Out—again?' Startled, she swung around to face him as he held open the vehicle door, his hand politely beneath her elbow as she climbed down. 'You mean, back to Les Saintes Maries?'

'No.' His eyes were hooded, enigmatic, as he held her bewildered gaze. 'If you must know, I am going to Marseille, and I may be late. Don't wait up.'

Marseille? Oh, no, not that! Tears suddenly stung Eve's eyes as she stared after him. His jaw had been terse, and he had looked at her as if he was already regretting not only his marriage but the subsequent turn it had taken. If he had wrung from her all the response he had hoped for the previous night, he obviously didn't like her reactions today. Whatever he had expected she had no means of knowing, and this must be his way of showing his disapproval. His way of demonstrating clearly that if he had turned briefly from Amélie it had only been a temporary deflection, a moment of madness, not to be repeated. This evening, he must be confident, Amélie would greet him with open arms!

Unhappiness lending an air of extreme exhaustion to her taut young face, Eve ran upstairs, almost forgetting in her misery to look in on the nursery, but Michel was by this time fast asleep. For a long moment she lingered, looking half enviously at his smoothly unconscious face before going to tell Marie that Raoul would not be in for dinner. She pretended not to notice as Marie glanced at her sharply. That Marie should even guess where he had gone would prove the final humiliation!

The remainder of the evening stretched long and dismal before her, and it was only just after ten when, unable to settle, Eve decided to go to bed with a book. In Raoul's study she had discovered a wide selection and chose a detective story, anything which might take her mind off her own problems. Yet, after a shower and the usual routine tasks necessary before retiring for the night, she still felt too restless to climb into bed, and for a moment lingered by her favourite spot at the window. A huge white moon sailed across the skies and, as she stared up at it, it sketched the poignant planes of her face in a transparent glow, highlighting the shadows, turning to silver the loose strands of hair where it touched. But, above all, it seemed to accentuate her solitary figure, bestowing a loneliness which she was almost beginning to feel deep down inside her.

Beyond the gardens, across the vast plains, the wind drifted softly with all the promise of an early summer, but, as on other nights, all was quiet. No voices of birds, no mistral washing wildly through the tops of the pines, only the faint hum of a wandering insect as it threw itself heedlessly against the glittering glass of the window, attracted by the soft flicker of light. There was so much about this part of France that was attractive, so much she liked, could learn to love, even as she loved the man who owned this large bit of it, given the chance. Tremulously Eve sighed. Before it had all seemed so easy, but she must have been a fool ever to think it really would be. How could she stay here now, loving Raoul the way she did, even for Michel's sake? The difficulty of hiding her true feelings might be, she conceded, an impossible task, and she dwelt despairingly on Raoul's acute embarrassment should he ever guess exactly how she felt about him.

So deep and hopeless were her thoughts that she didn't hear Marie's tentative knock until she tried again, this time louder.

Eve, thinking for one heart-stopping moment it was Raoul, hastily grabbed her white silk robe with its unmistakable stamp of Paris and slowly opened the door. Her pulse rate dropped to normal again as she saw it was only Marie—she might have known Raoul would never knock.

Marie was beset by her usual anxieties! 'Oh, *madame*,' she cried nervously, 'I wonder if you would mind looking at the child. He won't stop crying, I think he might be ill, and as *le maître* is—er—still out?'

'Of course.' Without pausing to satisfy Marie's curiosity about *le maître*, Eve followed Marie quickly down the corridor. It wasn't the first time since she had come here that Marie had sought her advice in the middle of the night, but for once Eve almost welcomed the diversion. It would quite probably be nothing serious, the young nursemaids had probably been indulging Michel too freely again, but Marie, excitable by nature, always seemed eager for reassurance.

Once in the nursery she found, as she had suspected, that Michel was suffering from a persistent pain in his small tummy. Swiftly she gathered him up, soothing him quietly before administering a small dose of something she kept for such occasions, to relieve it. It was only a matter of minutes before, cuddled closely in her arms, he went to sleep again.

'I'll stay with him a while longer,' she promised, sending Marie off to bed, together with the young nursemaid who slept in the adjoining room. As she laid the boy gently in his cot he turned over on his side, contented, and she doubted if he would wake again that night.

Carefully she turned his nightlight low and sat down in a chair by his side. Here she must have fallen asleep, as she woke with a start a little while later to find to her dismay Raoul standing by her side, watching her intently as she struggled to find her bemused senses. 'I must have forgotten where I was,' she gasped, but he merely smiled.

'Come, *ma chère*,' he said softly, bending over her, 'You must tell Marie she must manage herself occasionally when the child cries, but there is no need for you to stay any longer.'

So he had guessed what she had been doing. 'He had only a small pain,' she explained, 'nothing serious. However, Marie wasn't sure. I intended staying only a few minutes . . .'

'And you fell asleep? No matter,' he shrugged, bringing her to her feet, guiding her stumbling footsteps from the nursery, his arm gentle yet firm around her narrow waist. 'The child is all right now and we have much to discuss.'

'Raoul!' Outside the door, at once wholly awake, she pulled back from his arms, too conscious of the thinness of her robe, the diaphanous quality of the nightgown underneath. How could he expect her to behave rationally when he had only just returned from Marseille, from Amélie? 'I don't think we can have anything to talk about,' she exclaimed bitterly, her eyes huge in her white face. 'At least nothing that couldn't wait until the morning.'

'Shush, *ma chère*,' his voice soothed as his dark gaze slid deliberately over her slender figure, his grip on her waist tightening against her urgent struggles as he took her completely into his arms and kissed her hard. His hand moved slowly to her nape, threading through her ruffled hair, holding her passionately to him until she became completely acquiescent against him, his power over her no longer disputed.

Her lips throbbing, her body ablaze with a kind of feverish fire, Eve was scarcely aware of how she reached his study. She couldn't seem to fight him any more, nor could she count on any inclination to do so, common sense not seeming to function even slightly when up against an attraction such as his. 'Raoul!' From somewhere she tried to assert a small measure of independence, only to find herself pushed authoritatively down on to the wide velvet sofa, his hands lingering momentarily on her slim shoulders before he bent to switch on the electric fire. Again he took no notice of the wild note of entreaty in her voice.

'Stay there,' he commanded, leaving her to pour drinks, and bemused, Eve watched his every movement, staring at the back of his dark head, loving him too much, yet fully conscious that such one-sided emotion could bring her no happiness.

'Here, drink this, you are too pale, *ma chère*.' He was back by her side, placing a glass in her shaking hands, guiding it with his to her mouth, watching intently until she took a small sip. He dropped down beside her as she sat like a very fragile, curved statuette, unable, for some reason, to take her eyes off him.

Rather too quickly he half emptied his own glass, as if endeavouring to retain an equilibrium he felt was slipping. 'Darling,' it was the first time he had called her that and her skin tightened electrically, her cheeks colouring. Dropping her head to hide such rushing confusion didn't help. He noticed instantly, and his fingers went out to gently touch the vivid tide of it and stayed caressing beneath the vulnerable angle of her chin. 'Eve,' his voice deepened, 'you know where I've been this evening?'

'Yes,' she drew a painful steadying breath. There was nothing to be gained by pretending not to. 'You went to visit Amélie, and I think I know why.'

'You do?' He paused for one obviously baffled moment, his glance keen on the slight betraying quiver of her lips.

'Yes . . .' It just had to come out. 'You wish you had married her instead of me. Probably you've been to tell her so. There can be no other explanation.'

'Enough!' his voice whipped, his hand on her face tightening almost cruelly before relaxing again. 'I'm sorry, *ma chère*,' her intensely anguished expression acted as a brake, 'but of course you must be thinking something like this. It is natural, yet nothing was further from my mind.'

'You mean you don't love her?'

Smiling slightly, he shook his head. 'There is only one girl I love, my darling.' His fingers tensed, tilting up her chin, forcing her to look straight at him as he asked very softly, 'Can't you guess? From the moment I saw you . . .'

'No—Oh, Raoul!' Her voice came on a funny little gasp as he drew her forcibly to him, kissing her fiercely, as if glorying in the joy of her helplessly yielding body.

Minutes later he lifted his head. 'I love you,' he said, 'but before I tell you how much, we must talk about tonight. All the doubt between us must be cleared up, otherwise you will continue to fret. Do you recall, *ma chère*, when Mrs Wood gave me Amélie's lighter she also said when Amélie had left it? Something occurred to me almost immediately, but, to make sure, I checked up again with Mrs Wood while you finished your tea. Amélie had arrived at the hotel around five o'clock on the very day she had left you in the nature reserve. When she was supposed to be on her way back here to seek the forgotten picnic basket.'

'You mean . . .?' Eve flinched, her slight figure drooping as that dreadful experience came rushing back to her.

'I mean,' he went on swiftly, 'that all the time she has been lying. That while she was supposedly nursing her car off the reserve all the time she was at the hotel!'

'You're quite certain?' To Eve it didn't make sense.

Raoul's mouth thinned decisively. 'After checking with Mrs Wood I rang the garage where she left her car. The proprietor told me, *ma chère*, there was almost more sand in Amélie's petrol tank than the whole of the Sahara. Too much ever to have got there accidentally, and certainly more than would have allowed her to travel more than a very short distance. Of course he had no idea of the true circumstances, and I didn't tell him. *Mon dieu*,' Raoul ground out, 'and to think I didn't believe you!'

Her head came back against his shoulder, the tension inside her easing slightly. 'I would never lie to you, Raoul.'

'Darling,' his fingers played through her ruffled hair, tenderly, 'I've been a brute and must beg you to forgive me. It was Amélie who told me a tissue of lies, but it was actually my concern for you that made me so furious. This afternoon, as I pieced together what had really happened, I'm afraid I saw red. I was compelled to go and confront her personally—it would never be possible to pin Amélie down over the telephone, *petite*. I was so absolutely livid. To think she had endangered your life, spending that evening in Mrs Wood's hotel in order to give you a fright! And, on top of this, she confessed everything when I found her in Marseille, and wasn't in any way repentant, even when I told her that what she had done could easily have been construed as a kind of premeditated murder.'

'Oh, no!' Eve's eyes flew to his, startled. 'I think she would only intend giving me a fright. Something to make me hate the Camargue and hurry back to London.'

'Even so she couldn't have guaranteed your safety. She must certainly be a little mad. I will never have her back here!'

'I think,' shuddering, Eve swallowed, trying not to exaggerate, 'I think she could, on occasion, act very irresponsibly.'

'Unbalanced?' He halted narrowly, an odd unexpected note in his voice. 'Was this why you decided to marry me, *ma chère*?'

Inconsequently, Eve tried to avoid a direct answer. 'Poor Amélie,' she sighed. 'She had no idea I'd ever worked for Mrs Wood, or even stayed in her hotel. If we hadn't gone there today ...'

'Eve—I asked you a question.' There was a wealth of male purpose behind his voice.

'Yes,' Eve answered evasively, 'it was on my mind at the time.'

'And since then?'

Her heart beating suddenly too fast, she turned a delicate profile to him. 'Since then, Raoul,' she confessed, frantically, 'I've been fighting a losing battle, trying not to face the fact that I loved you. Then last night...' her breath changed as emotion shot through her, accentuating her extreme pallor.

'Yes?' he prompted, his hand sliding over the silk of her shoulder lightly, but enough to break the sharp sense of discipline which held her.

She turned up her face, knowing he didn't have to force her to surrender. 'Last night,' she whispered tremulously, 'I realised how much...'

Silently he held her to him, his heart striking into her with force, his lips warm against the throbbing nerve at her temple. 'Before I kiss you, *mignonne*, because I may not be able to stop, there are still one or two things left to say. On our wedding day, Céleste said something about sending for you. I'm afraid the manner of your arrival here was no longer important. It was something I had long put from me, certainly something I hadn't the time or inclination to think about on my wedding day. But was that also true, my darling. You let me think you had arrived completely uninvited. To protect Céleste you chose not to say anything?'

'Yes.' There was in Eve a fine recklessness, compelling her to confess all. Perhaps, if Raoul really loved her, he had to hear it? 'Céleste threatened that if I didn't come she would bring Michel to London. Unfortunately, when I did arrive she had mixed up the dates. I had her letter, but she had lost mine and hadn't made a note of my arrival. This was why I came here. My money was running out and I felt it imperative to know what had gone wrong. She had especially asked me not to telephone, in case...' Her voice trailed off, unwilling to implicate Céleste any further.

'In case,' Raoul supplied, with a wry flicker of humour, 'I found out. And I suppose,' he added, still wryly, 'in retrospect I couldn't really blame her. And, when you did come, I couldn't get rid of you quick enough.'

'You threw me out, literally.' The reproach in her voice was audible.

Raoul's laughter was low. 'So you once said, *madame*, and again I apologise, but perhaps you don't understand how desperate I was to be rid of you. Immediately I caught sight of you I sensed you were a threat to my peace of mind. Not that I was wholly convinced you actually were whom you said you were, but how could I welcome you after protesting so much about Carol? Then the next time I saw you and held you in my arms I knew I could never let you go.'

Through the uneven beating of a feverish pulse she forced herself to ask, 'You never told me why you never liked Carol or her family.'

In his voice was a half impatient tenderness. 'It was nothing really personal, *ma petite*. Perhaps you were not aware that Dominique was already betrothed to a French girl when he ran off with your cousin. Can you imagine what I, a mere man, was left to cope with? The weeping of a distracted, deserted fiancée, a necessity to calm and appease irate parents. I may have over-reacted, but the fact that my brother, whom I relied on a lot, didn't return for almost two months did not help. *Mon dieu*,' Raoul smiled, 'but I was ready to hate the lot of you!'

'But Carol?' Eve protested.

Raoul's smile faded and he sighed. 'Oh, we got on very well, my darling, eventually, but she did little to help Dominique settle down. Always they were off somewhere, or doing something unnecessary, such as refurbishing the old hut down by the lagoon in such a way that one dared scarcely put a foot inside it. We used it a lot at one time for watching wild life on the water.'

Eve remembered, with a quiver, which prompted her to

say when otherwise she might not, 'You certainly didn't approve when she went to Rhodesia!'

'It wasn't exactly that,' Raoul explained curtly. 'They had only just returned from America, and there was a lot to do.'

'Yet Carol wasn't well?'

'You sound surprised, *ma chère*,' he shrugged wryly. 'I think Carol often made a convenience of her health. Usually she was quite fit.'

'And this is why you wanted to keep Michel here when his parents died. So that he might have a stable home??'

'Something like that, *ma chère*.' Raoul looked at her contemplatively. 'Anyway, we shall see. After we return from our honeymoon his grandparents will come on a long visit, so we will not worry too much about the future right now, *mignonne*.'

'A honeymoon...?' Was his voice full of the old tantalising mockery, or did he really mean it? She was never quite sure where she was with him. Her hand clung suddenly to the dark silk of his dressing gown, her face taut with extreme sensitivity as she gave an odd little shudder.

'Need you ask?' He understood the query in her voice and his own was tolerant. 'I've been getting everything organised. I find I can't wait until Céleste returns from America to have you completely to myself. There is a small villa I own in the Swiss Alps, which isn't so far away. I know you will adore it.'

'Oh, Raoul!' The prospect in front of her seemed so dazzling that she could scarcely accept it without being prone to some doubt. Not for herself—she could never question the strength of her own feelings, but what of his? 'How can you be sure,' she felt helplessly forced to go on, 'how can you be sure I'll settle down any better than Carol?'

'Because I do, my darling.' His arm curved hard as it tightened about her. 'In fact, merely from watching you since you first came, I can almost guarantee it. But, whether you do or not, it's a risk I must take. Besides, *ma chère*,' a glint of dry humour flickered through his eyes, 'is it not rather late to be thinking of this now?'

'But——' she began uncertainly, a small devil of perversity driving her.

'No more buts, *petite*.' Decisively his lips cut off whatever words she had been about to utter. 'Don't you think,' he murmured, a slightly roughened edge to his voice, 'we've talked enough for one night? Nothing can really matter any more but this, *ma belle enfant*. This will last for ever!' Closely he held her, his mouth lingering on the wide curve of her lips before sliding over the soft silk of her throat, lingering for one threatening moment on the wildly beating pulse before seeking the warm skin of her shoulder, the fragrant appeal of her seductive young body.

'For ever . . .' There was an unconscious break in her voice as she said it, wholly submissive as she pressed his dark head lovingly to her breast, no thought inside her of denying him any longer. It was a word that would be stamped indelibly on her heart for always. That and this place, this man, with whom she would always be wholly content.

YOU'LL L♥VE
Harlequin Magazine

for women who enjoy reading fascinating stories of exciting romance in exotic places

SUBSCRIBE NŌW!

This is a colorful magazine especially designed and published for the readers of Harlequin novels.

Now you can receive your very own copy delivered right to your home every month throughout the year for only 75¢ an issue.

This colorful magazine is available only through Harlequin Reader Service, so enter your subscription now!

In every issue...

Here's what you'll find:

♥ a complete, full-length romantic novel...illustrated in color.

♥ exotic travel feature...an adventurous visit to a romantic faraway corner of the world.

♥ delightful recipes from around the world...to bring delectable new ideas to your table.

♥ reader's page...your chance to exchange news and views with other Harlequin readers.

♥ other features on a wide variety of interesting subjects.

Start enjoying your own copies of Harlequin magazine immediately by completing the subscription reservation form.

Not sold in stores!

Harlequin Presents...

By popular demand...
24 original novels from this series—by 7 of the world's greatest romance authors.

These back issues have been out of print for some time. So don't miss out; order your copies now!

Harlequin Reader Service
ORDER FORM